The PARADIGM SHIFT of ELIZABETH ANN

Volume Two: The Elizabeth Ann Trilogy

J. NICHOLS MOWERY

THE PARADIGM SHIFT OF ELIZABETH ANN
Volume Two: The Elizabeth Ann Trilogy

iUniverse books may be ordered through booksellers or by contacting:

iUniverse
1663 Liberty Drive
Bloomington, IN 47403
www.iuniverse.com
1-800-Authors (1-800-288-4677)

ISBN: 978-1-4917-9061-8 (sc)
ISBN: 978-1-4917-9062-5 (e)

Library of Congress Control Number: 2016904050

Print information available on the last page.

iUniverse rev. date: 03/22/2016

CONTENTS

Prologue vii

Chapter 1   June 1st—Liz. 1

Chapter 2   June 1st—Beth 15

Chapter 3   June 1st—Eliza 30

Chapter 4   June 5th—Liz 44

Chapter 5   June 5th—Beth 55

Chapter 6   June 5th—Eliza 67

Chapter 7   June 10th—Liz 74

Chapter 8   June 10th—Beth 86

Chapter 9   June 10th—Eliza 108

Chapter 10   June 15th—Liz 115

Chapter 11   June 15th—Beth 123

Chapter 12   June 15th—Eliza's Last Morning 135

Chapter 13   June 20th—The Summer Solstice 143

August Epiloge 157

PROLOGUE

It was a perfect metaphysical moment when the alignment of planets and stars created a massive astrological rupture in the Universe which forced life path dimensions to experience a true quantum leap. Within nanoseconds, the eruption of the energy fields in the Universal Plains forced atoms to split and fracture into massive energy waves causing phenomenal paranormal movements. At that moment, like-kind dimensions were forced apart from their axis to mesh together at common focused points on the Universal Plain.

As these dimensions skewed and joined with their like-kind parallel dimensions, they overlapped and intertwined to interlock at places known to each like-kind Parallel Life from childhood to adulthood. This was the phenomenon which brought the dimensions of the Parallel Lives of Elizabeth Ann Anderson together at the focused point of the golden stone in the floor of their cabins at Redcliff's Beach in Washington State along the Pacific Ocean.

James Anderson built the original cabin for his family, his wife Jill and daughters, two year old Dana Marie and new born Elizabeth Ann. It is then that James was directed by the Universe to place a piece of the large agate within the north cliff face into the cement floor of his cabin. During their childhood, his children played around the glowing stone where it lay under the dining table. It would be there where the three Elizabeth Ann Andersons, Liz Day, Beth Anderson and Eliza Staples, would meet each other on the first of June many years later.

On that June first, each of the three Parallel Lives of Elizabeth Ann suffered a traumatic tragedy at two in the afternoon. These tragedies caused their like-kind dimensions to intertwine at the focus point of the golden agate and changed their lives forever.

On that June first, at two in the afternoon, Liz Day's husband, Peter, flew his small plane into thick fog and crashed in the Olympic Mountains.

On that June first, at two in the afternoon, Beth Anderson's life-partner, Maxine Oakley, died after a long battle with ovarian cancer.

On that June first, at two in the afternoon while in a medicated haze, Eliza Staples shot and killed her ex-husband, Jack Staples and her best friend.

In the following weeks, each Elizabeth Ann met other women within their home who looked exactly as they did and each woman claimed the space of their father's original cabin as their own. After several such encounters, the three women began to realize they were Parallel Lives of one original child named Elizabeth Ann Anderson.

When each accepted their paranormal connection, the three women became aware that more than their physical likeness tied them to the others. As the Summer Solstice approached, each woman faced horrific events which nearly took their lives. When they met again at the adjoined dining tables over the golden stone, the Parallel Lives of Elizabeth Ann realized whatever effected one of them effected the others. At that time, the three determined to make positive choices in the future.

At the beginning of their second year together, the three Elizabeth Anns meet at their adjoined tables over the large golden agate in the polished cement floor of their cabins. Each accepts Beth Anderson as the original child named Elizabeth Ann Anderson due to the golden agate bowl given to her at the south cliffs.

ONE

June 1ˢᵗ—Liz

L I Z runs along the edge of the waves towards the north cliffs with a determination and sense of purpose which she hasn't had for some time. This morning will be the last time she will speak to her dead husband, Peter Day, while standing before the touchstone within the cliff face. These talks started after his death as they helped her work through the anger and pain she'd felt about his lying, as to who he was and the man he'd actually been, during their thirty year marriage.

Just as she steps onto the huge granite slab, the sun breaks over the Coastal Mountain range and momentarily blinds Liz. Closing her eyes against the brightness, she waits for her eyes to adjust and hears the raucous screams of hundreds of seabirds lifting off their aeries along the cliff face. Looking up, Liz watches the swarm soar out to the western horizon. It is then she sees a thick morning mist flowing off the Pacific and rapidly covering the beach.

Turning to face the golden stone in the cliff face, she rubs its glowing surface as she remembers those who are no longer with her, "I am determined to no longer mourn the past or for what could have been and will only look to the future. My Parallel Lives, Beth Anderson and Eliza

1

Staples are my family now and we meet daily at the adjoined tables. I thank you for bringing them to me, Peter. I thank you for the money you hid which I found. It has given me freedom to control my life as never before. I quit my job at Travel Magazine and am writing the story of Elizabeth Ann's Parallel Lives. It begins the day each of us lost our loved one. I tell how you died, how you lied and how those lies impacted my life. Mostly though, it will be about how the Elizabeth Anns experience their lives, alone and together, since that first day. Though it is a true story, I call it fiction for I don't want others to know that it's a true story. When I discovered you weren't the person I thought you were all the years of our marriage, Peter, I became filled with anger. Over the past year, my Parallel Lives have helped me remember there were as many good things as the bad."

Liz leans towards the glowing stone and presses her forehead to it, staying there as she silently thinks of the family she'd lost and loved so deeply. When she turns towards the beach, a soft whining noise seems to come from the right side of the stone slab. Peering into the fog, she sees a large filthy dog at the edge of the large stone. The cur looks at her with soft pleading eyes that shine a dull golden color. Slowly the pitiful animal creeps closer and lays its head near her feet.

Seeing how scrawny and covered with bloody wounds the animal is, Liz holds out her right hand to let the dog sniff her fingers. As it does, its stringy curl of a tail wags over its back. "Oh, you poor pitiful thing. What ever happened to you? Who would beat and starve you so terribly?"

When the dog's dry nose touches her hand, Liz stares into the animal's golden eyes and it heaves a big sigh. The site of such a scraggly animal touches a need deep within Liz and she pats the matted fur on its head. Gently rubbing the grime off its muzzle, she slides her hands down the animal's back and gasps at how deep some of the gashes are. Touching the matted blood, she sees both fresh cuts and old scars. Sickened, Liz realizes the dog has been badly abused over a long period of time.

Lifting its snout with her hand, Liz looks into its golden eyes and a soft pinkish grey tongue flicks out to give a quick swipe of approval.

At that moment, Liz loses her heart to the forlorn beast and says, "Hey, kiddo, you've had a hell of a time of it, haven't you? I'm so glad you found me. I've been wanting a dog for some time and it seems you've chosen me. Want to come home with me? I'll feed you then we'll get a vet to look at those terrible gashes down your back. I want to see you beautiful again. Who would ever do these things to such a fine dog?"

As she talks to the animal, she continues to rub the grime off its head and the animal slowly inches closer. When Liz doesn't move away, the animal presses up against her right leg and again heaves a sigh. Then the dog looks up at her with a wrinkled nose grin and its eyes flash with golden lights. As she bends to check over the animal, Liz grabs hold of the protruding touchstone with her left hand to keep from tipping too far.

In that instant, a rush of energy pours from the touchstone, pulses through Liz and shoots out her right hand onto the dog's head. Instantly, the animal is covered by a golden aura and begins to shake violently from the tip of its nose to the end of its tail. With each violent shake, the dog's appearance changes and, the filthy scrawny cur that laid itself at Liz's feet, becomes a strong beautiful animal with a thick silken coat standing beside her.

In those seconds, all the cuts and injuries on the dog's back heal and the deep scars are hidden under the thick coat of tawny fur. As the dog changes, Liz is unable to let go of the touchstone or the dog's head. All she can do is watch with amazement. Soon black accent hairs form around its eyes, down the middle of its back and into the fluff of its tail that now curls high over its back.

When the changes to the animal are complete, the shaking stops as abruptly as it began. Now a beautiful healthy dog stands in front of Liz and looks boldly into her eyes. At that moment, the dog barks three times and spins in tight circles, bouncing with excitement. Laughing, Liz hugs the animal and runs her hands through its thick fur trying to find the old wounds. What she finds is a tight leather cord cutting deeply into the animal's neck. Giving the thin old leather a yank, it snaps in two and drops to the granite slab.

Picking up the pieces, Liz exclaims, "Someone tied this on you when you a puppy and never changed it. My friend, I'm so glad you came to the beach and found me. You must have been so frightened."

As she smiles down at the dog, the animal returns a wide wrinkled nosed grin that pulls its muzzle up over its teeth. Laughing, Liz says, "Let's get rid of this old thing. I'll buy you a new one in town."

However, when she starts to fling the old leather into the waves, the pieces change into a wide shiny green leather collar with silver studs and a silver buckle at one end. Stunned, she holds it out to the dog and asks, "Look... it's a new collar. Do you like it?"

Yes.

Startled by the word coming into her head, Liz pulls back and asks the dog, "Did you just say yes to this new collar?"

Yes, I did. Please, put it on me.

His words so unsettle Liz that she quickly buckles the collar around the dog's neck, then stands back to see what else might happen. When nothing more does, she says, "Well, it certainly looks good on you. Welcome to your new life, my friend. Should I name you or do you have one already?"

I am called Kip.

When Kip's answer comes in her head, Liz looks into the dog's golden eyes and says, "Of course, it would be Kip. That's Norse for King, isn't it? What else would you be called? You certainly are kingly, my friend. That's for sure. It's very nice to meet you, Kip. I'm Liz Day. I'm so glad you came here today. We're going to be great friends. I've wanted a good dog and you found me."

Hi, Liz.

"Hi, Kip. Everything about you is amazing. I believe you're a breed of dog known as an Elkhound. Does your collar fit all right or would you like me to take it off?"

I like it. Thank you for putting it on me.

"Well, it certainly looks beautiful on you. Now let's head home."

As the two trot along the line of foam left by the last wave, they dodge beachgoers coming out of the fog. All along Shoreline Drive, lights blink on and off in houses that sit high above the sand dunes covering the six miles of beach. Smiling, she wonders if any of those neighbors saw the changes made on the dog running beside her and thinks,

What would they think if they knew I also hear him answer me?

Don't worry, Liz, we are beyond the judgement of Earthlings.

As these words are so unexpected, Liz truly doesn't hear them and continues to run with the animal trotting beside her. When she hears the snapping of a flag, she peers through the fog, but is unable to see the flagpole. That stops Liz and she says to the dog, "Hear that, Kip? It's the flag on the flagpole Peter setup years ago so we'd know where to turn whenever the fog too thick. Turn towards the sound. The path through the dunes is where the pole stands. We're home."

When she reaches the steps up to the deck around her home, Liz finds Kip sitting next to the sliding glass door. When she opens the door, the dog barks three times and spins in tight joyful circles. Liz grabs the happy animal and kisses the top of the animal's head, saying, "Darling, Kip, it's so lovely having you run with me. We're going to do that every morning and become the best of friends. Just think how many adventures we'll have, Kip."

More than you can ever imagine.

When his words come into her head, Liz looks into the dog's eyes and sees an intelligence that almost scares her. Rubbing the place she'd just kissed, she says, "This boney bump between your ears is called the 'bump of knowledge' and yours certainly shows what a smart animal you are. When I saw your wounds heal as the touchstone's energy flowed into you, I knew you were very special. Do you hurt anywhere?"

No, I am healed. The pain is gone. Thank you, my friend.

"You are most welcome, Kip. I'll take you to the vet in town this afternoon so you can get the immunization shots you should have. Do you know if your other person ever had you immunized?"

No, never. I'm sure of that.

"I'll take you to the new vet in Ocean Shores after we eat lunch. Those scars are deep and I want the vet to see them in case your old master comes at me and tries to get you back. Were you chained so you couldn't run away?"

Yes. It finally broke and I ran away to find you.

Going straight into the kitchen, Liz takes a steel pan from a cupboard, fills it with water and places it on the floor Kip to drink. After that she pulls out the leftover meatloaf from the night before, cuts a slice off for herself and breaks the rest into a bowl setting it next to the pan of water.

When she carries her lunch to the dining table, she sees Kip still sitting outside the open door. Liz says, "Kip, come in here. This is your home from now on. There's a water dish and meatloaf over there in the kitchen. It's all I have until I get to the store and buy some good kibble. The veterinarian's office is right across the street from the IGA. I'll shop there after we see him."

While they're eating, Liz hears shouts coming through the open slider door and realizes the sound comes from the house to the north of hers. Looking out the window, she sees a man on the house's deck who seems to be shouting into one hand and pointing up the beach with the other. Lifting the binoculars off their peg next to the door frame, Liz steps out to the deck and scans the north beach.

Seeing nothing unusual on the beach or in the high incoming waves, she raises the glasses up along the cliff face and sees a lone woman crouched on one of the highest ledges. "That's what he sees. The stupid woman got too close to the terns' nests up there and is being attacked by them."

As Liz watches, angry seabirds swoop down at the woman, again and again. Trying to fend them off, the woman holds a large camera over her head with one hand and waves a notebook with her other as she slowly backs away.

Amazed, Liz makes a mental note to find out who that woman is and says to Kip, "At least the woman's holding her own. Terns are fiercely protective avian parents and can do a lot of damage to anyone silly enough to mess with their nests."

Feeling a cold nose nudge her bare leg, Liz looks down at the dog's wise face. "I agree, it's time we get to the vet's for your checkup and shots. I'm sure you're healthy, but I don't want you to catch anything you can get immunized against."

Yes, vaccines are good. Distemper and rabies are very bad.

Again, Liz stares into the animal's eyes and says, "I'm beginning to think you are a very old soul, Kip. You must keep telling me what I should know if I don't seem to know what I should. Understand?"

However, the dog doesn't answer. Instead, he goes to stand in front of the door into the garage and looks back at her. Shaking her head with a chuckle, Liz opens the door and Kip trots to the passenger side of the car. When she opens that door, the dog jumps onto the seat and watches her climb behind the steering wheel. His eyes never leave her as she pushes the remote to open the garage door and backs the car onto the driveway. However, the moment she turns onto Shoreline Drive and is heading down the straightaway, Kip lays his chin on her right leg and heaves a loud sigh. Smiling, Liz scratches behind his ears and feels a sense of well-being that she's not had for a long while.

As she slows to a stop at the four way in Ocean Shores, the dog wakens, sits up and watches Liz turn the car to the left and drive the car down the street toward the IGA. Suddenly, she turns into a park area and stops in an open space near a sign saying 'The Office of Dr. Dan Parker, Veterinarian'. Then he watches as she gets out of the car and hurries around to open the passenger door.

However, when she opens the passenger door expecting him to jump out, Kip hesitates and looks towards the street, growling low in his throat. Turning to see what causes this reaction, she notices an old battered white pick-up truck moving slowly along the street. When the driver looks their way, Kip bristles visibly and growls menacingly even though the truck turns into the IGA parking lot across the road.

"Come, Kip. Don't be afraid that man. Let's go into the office building. That person will never hurt you again. I promise you that."

Hurrying through the front door of the office, Liz stops at the reception desk and Kip sits next to her feet. The woman at the desk is typing at a computer, so Liz waits until she finishes. However, before she can say a word, Kip growls loudly and takes a stiff legged stance in front of Liz. A second later, the entry door bangs open and a seedy looking man barges into the office glaring at her and the dog.

Instantly. Kip backs against her legs and snarls loudly. "Hush, boy. Hush. Kip. Sit, Kip. Stay. That man can't hurt you ever again." Hearing her voice, the dog settles against her legs and the man moves to sit in a chair across the room. All the while he does, Kip bares his teeth and growls deep in his throat.

Reaching down, Liz snags the dog's collar with her left hand and sees that the dog's hackles have risen down the middle of his back. Holding onto the wide collar, Liz holds him to her and speaks loudly, "Quiet, Kip. That man isn't going to hurt you ever again." To the receptionist, she says, "We've come to see the doctor. I don't have an appointment and Kip only needs vaccinations."

Still pressing against her legs, the dog stares across the room and growls. When the man stands and moves to a chair closer to the reception desk, Kip pushes against Liz's legs so hard that she has to step backwards. It's then that she feels the dog's trembling and Liz shouts at the man, "Stay where you are, mister. I don't know if you're the person who beat this dog before he came to me, but he sure hates the sight and smell of you. So stop where you are or go back out that door, fast."

At that, the man returns to the chair in the far corner of the room and glares at the dog. Kip says to Liz,

It's him. He's the one who beat me.

Before Liz can respond, the young receptionist at the desk says, "Lady, what's going on with your dog? You should have a lead on him. Here, use this one today but get your own before you come again and bring this one back. Use a lead whenever you come to see the Doctor. Do you have an appointment?"

"No. Kip came to me badly beaten and scrawny. Now that he's healed and strong, I want him to get vaccinated for everything. Also I want him checked for other injuries. I'm sorry he's growling. He's reacting to that mean looking man over there. Kip seems to hate the sight of him. I think he's the person who beat Kip so terribly."

As Liz speaks, the receptionist checks her computer, then says,

"Looks as if you're in luck. We've a cancellation for an operation scheduled this afternoon. You'll have to wait a few more minutes though, as the doctor is with another patient. Let's take Kip into the prep room. You'll have to stay with him during the examination and while the shots are given."

"Of course." Liz replies as she leads Kip to the door which the woman has opened for them.

Suddenly, the angry man moves across the room, yelling, "Hey lady, that's my dog you got there. Chukka, get over here. Now."

Turning from the door into the prep room, Liz sees that the man now holds a length of chain and is swinging it towards them. "I said, that's my dog, lady, that's my Chukka. Come, Chukka, come here, you damn bastard."

When the man takes one step towards them, Kip lunges at him, snapping his teeth wildly and moving so fast that the lead slips through Liz's hands. As the dog leaps, the man throws himself backwards and loses his grip on the length of heavy chain which flies across the room to crash against a door on the other side of the reception desk. Almost immediately, a tall grey haired man in surgical clothes rushes out and demands, "What the hell is going on out here? Who threw this length of chain in here?"

So focused on the man in front of her, Liz doesn't hear his words, as she's holding Kip's lead with both hands and shouting, "Stay where you are, you son of a bitch, or I'll unleash this dog and let him meet you on equal terms for a change. Anyone can see that Kip hates you and wants to tear you to shreds. Yes, I believe you. This dog was yours. That's why he's trying to get to you and kill you. You must have done terrible things to this animal. Now that you no longer control him, he seems to want to even things up. Kip was a poor pathetic wreck of an animal when he came to me. You stay way back or you'll feel every bit of the hatred he has for you and I won't try to stop him."

Without turning her head, Liz shouts, "Miss, get that damn vet out here. Right now. Move it!"

Instantly, a man's calm voice says, "I'm Dr. Dan Parker and I'm right behind you. Can you hold your dog while I walk that man out the office door?"

Seeing Liz's nod, the veterinarian walks directly to the angry man, talks softly to him, then both move to and through the front door. As the door closes behind them, the dog settles back against Liz's legs and she says, "Good dog. Good Kip. Stay close to me, boy. You're safe now. That terrible man is gone. He'll never hurt you again."

The sound of her voice calms the dog and he settles between Liz's feet still watching the door into the office. When nothing more happens, his hackles slowly relax along his spine and he heaves a big sigh. Whispering to him, Liz says, "You're safe with me, Kip. No one will ever beat you again. I love you, darling dog. You're mine and no one will ever hurt you again."

It's then that Dr. Parker comes back into the office and smiles at the women, "Hopefully, we won't see that guy again. Man, oh, man, he is one mean son of a gun."

Nodding to the receptionist, he says, "If that guy comes back, call the police. Don't hesitate. He made all sorts of threats, at the dog, at this lady and at me. He claims you stole his dog. When I said I doubted that very much, I thought he was going to strangle me. Luckily, several people are on the sidewalk watching some cops handle a fender bender down the block."

Looking at Liz, he says, "Bring your dog into the prep room and I'll check him over. Even through his thick coat, I can see someone did a lot of damage to this guy. Those deep scars didn't happen by accident."

As Liz and Kip start to follow the doctor into the prep room, the glass entry door slams open and the same man rushes towards them, shouting, "That's my dog, you damned bitch. He's mine. Chukka get over here, come. Chukka, come."

Then, the man lunges towards them and the vet yells, "Doris, dial 911. Get the cops here. Now."

Reaching past Liz, Dr. Dan Parker grabs the raging man by the neck of his shirt and pushes him away from the women, yelling, "Mister, I am Dan Parker, owner of this business and you're trespassing. Did your dog look like this dog or was he filthy and scrawny with lots of wounds from your beatings? There are laws about beating animals. Now get your sorry ass out that door, right now, or I'll press charges. Get out, now! The police are on their way and if you aren't gone by the time they get here, I'll press all the charges I can think of against you."

Instead of leaving, the man swings a fist at Parker, who deflects the punch with his left arm and pushes the man towards the entry door. As they move, the man pulls away and swings at the vet again. Blocking the man's attack, Parker holds tight to the man's jacket and the two men wrestle each other across the room. Slipping and sliding on the slate tiles, they spin around and move back towards the entry door. It's then that the angry man twists around and swings wildly at the veterinarian, stumbles and trips over his own feet. Then, as if in slow motion, the man falls backwards and lands with a bounce flat on his back on the slate tiled floor. First his body lands with a whump, then his head hits hard with a loud bonk and the man lies still.

Immediately, Dr. Parker reaches down, grabs the man's jacket front and yanks him onto his feet. Then half carrying and half dragging the dazed man out the front door, Parker takes the man across the street to where the old pickup is parked. The two women in the office watch out the front windows and see Dr. Parker push the man into the front seat of the truck, slam the truck door and walk back across the street.

As Parker reaches for the office door, the man opens the truck's door and yells something. Instead of responding, Dr. Parker hurries into the office to where the two women and dog wait. Then, they all watch through the window as the angry man staggers out from the pick-up, shakes his fist towards the vet's office and shouts something. Seeing him do this, Liz hisses, "He's coming back. He's coming back. Lock the door. Please, lock the door."

However, in the next few seconds, the angry man stumbles to the curb shaking his fist at the three people in the office window and, without looking left or right, steps directly into the path of a UPS delivery truck speeding up the street. The truck's impact throws the man's body high in the air where it flips once before landing onto the tailgate of that same old white pickup. Bent nearly in half, the body hangs half in and half out, as if a discarded puppet.

The very second of the impact, Liz hears the delivery truck's brakes scream to a stop several feet down the street. In the next moment, the driver jumps from the truck's open door and screams frantically at the cops handling the fender bender down the block. Then the driver runs to the front of her truck and looks around it for whatever it was she hit. Finally, a bystander points to the body dangling over the truck's tailgate. Then the deliverywoman screams and screams until she vomits again.

The two policemen handling the fender-bender jump into their patrol car and, with lights flashing, move their patrol car directly beside the delivery truck, blocking the street to all other traffic. One officer runs to the sobbing truck driver and escorts her to the rear seat of the patrol car. The other officer clears the onlookers, gathered around the tailgate, staring at the blank grey face of the once angry man.

Watching it all, Dr. Parker tells the receptionist, "Those policemen may come in to get a statement. If they do, come get me. I'm going to give this dog his check up and immunization shots. Please, follow me..." Then he exclaims, "Oh damn, looks like that cop is heading in here now. You three wait here. I'll be back shortly. Stay inside."

After he's left the office, Liz kneels beside Kip and hugs the quivering animal close to her trying to calm both their trembling. Through the glass doorway, the two women see an ambulance pull into the parking lot of the IGA. When it parks next to the white pickup, three EMTs get out and position a gurney next to the dangling body on the white truck. Two of the EMT's lift the body off the tailgate and the third pushes the gurney under it, then covers it with a sheet.

When the gurney is slid into the ambulance, Liz takes Kip into the prep room to wait for Dr. Parker and says, "This time, it's really over, Kip. That awful man will never hurt you or anyone else ever again. You're safe, my darling dog, and you belong to me from now on. Is that okay with you, boy?"

Instead of an answer, the dog presses himself against her and sighs loudly. This time, the receptionist reaches down to pet the animal's head, "This guy sure has a big contented sigh. Does he always do that when you talk to him about something?"

Liz nods and silently thanks Kip for coming to her. This time, she is no longer surprised when Kip answers,

You are most welcome, dear Liz. We are both lucky I finally found you.

A few moments later, Dr. Dan Parker comes into the room, sees her holding Kip and says, "You've got a wonderful dog there, Mrs. Day. He was very lucky to have found you. I'd guess you two are meant to be together. As I always say, animals choose us, not the other way around. I'm happy for you both. How about I get those shots done and check to see if those old scars are going to give him trouble in the future."

Liz smiles and says, "Thank you so much for what you've done for us today, Dr. Parker. That terrible man saw us come in here and followed us. His old truck pulled into that parking lot when Kip and I were coming up your sidewalk. I can't thank you enough for helping us today."

"You're most welcome, Mrs. Day. I'm glad I was here to stop him from harming you or your dog. Doris, please tell the people in room three that I'll be with them in a few minutes. If they ask what the holdup is, tell them what happened, but only if they ask. Don't take too much time from the desk."

Then he turns to Liz and says, "Kip's shots will take just a few minutes and his checkup should go quickly. You've done a great job bringing him back to health. You'll soon be on your way home, Mrs. Day."

Liz replies, "Please, call me Liz, Dr. Parker. Mrs. Day was my mother-in-law and both she and my husband are long gone."

Smiling, Dan Parker answers, "Okay, Liz, I will if you'll call me Dan. I feel we three must become friends after all that's happened today."

As he says this, he kneels beside Kip and quickly administers the needed shots in the dog's shoulder and hip. "Good, boy, Kip. You're such a fine dog, I hope you and I become great friends. Would you persuade your mistress to have dinner with me sometime soon?"

Then Parker looks up at Liz and says, "How about it?"

Surprised at the man's request, Liz looks sideways at Kip and hears,

Say yes.

Liz laughs as the dog pulls away from the vet's hold and shakes vigorously. "He says I should say yes."

Dr. Parker smiles and gives Kip a good rubdown. Then the dog says to Liz,

Make it soon, I like this man.

Patting the dog, Liz says coyly, "It seems Kip wants to see you soon, so pick me up at six tonight."

This time, it is Dr. Parker who looks surprised and he says, "I know I said he's quite a dog, but don't tell me he actually speaks to you and you hear him?"

"Only on important matters." Liz grins.

Tilting his head, Dan Parker smiles and asks, "Did he really give permission for you to go out to dinner with me?"

Yes. Good man.

Liz replies, "Oh yes, Dr. Parker, Kip thinks you're a good man and that I should go out with you. However, your question was to me, so I'll answer for myself. I'd like very much to have dinner with you. What day and time will you pick me up?"

Dan Parker chuckles, "Tonight? As you said, I'll be at your place at six tonight. Where will I find the two of you?"

"We're at the north end of Redcliff's Beach. It's the place along the beach with all the trees and a weathered copper roof."

"I know the place. I have friends that live in the house just north of your place. The Jacksons bring injured birds or other animals to me every so often. Larry and Mary are doing studies on the flora and fauna for the state of Washington."

Liz laughs and says, "Well that certainly answers a lot of questions about the woman. She was climbing all over the cliffs, taking photos of birds, this morning. Right now, though, I've got to go to the IGA for Kip's food. See you at six."

TWO

June 1ˢᵗ—Beth

BETH stares at the large agate bowl sitting on her dining table and remembers the terrible storm that nearly tore her cabin apart one year ago. After her insurance man lined up a cleanup crew and a heavy equipment operator, they cleared the float logs and debris from her house. While they did that, she hiked the south beach to find her things washed away by the crashing waves of that perfect storm.

This morning, Beth realizes that if the love of her life, Maxine Oakley, had not died days before the storm, both Maxine and the hospital bed she laid upon would have been crushed by the massive logs that crashed through the glass slider door and windows. Now the dining table is back where it belongs over the golden stone in the floor in front of a new bank of windows and Beth sits in her chair facing the ocean.

Suddenly her cat, Dandelion, leaps onto the table and circles the golden bowl which sets in the middle of the long table, directly over the golden stone in the floor below. Tracing her fingers around the rim of the large glowing bowl, she follows the cat and the resulting humming from the agate bowl fills her mind with the memory of how the bowl came to be hers the day of the wild storm.

Told to keep out of her house as the crews did their work, she took the beach sled her father had made and headed towards the south cliffs to find her things. After placing any usable item above the high tide line to dry, her plan was to retrieve them on the trip home. When she reached the south cliffs around noon, she took a water and food break at the south cliffs. It was then that a massive hunk fell off the granite cliffs and exposed a huge protruding agate that looked exactly as the touchstone in the north cliff face.

After the dust settled, Beth climbed onto the debris to get a close look at the glorious stone. When she reached up and touched the translucent stone, a large hollow hunk broke off the stone's face and dropped into her hands. At that same moment, she was told to place it on the dining table directly over the golden stone in the floor of her cabin. It was also the moment that Beth was told that she was the original child named Elizabeth Ann Anderson.

Every morning since, as she sits before the beautiful glowing bowl of agate, Beth receives messages from the golden bowl and the stones within the north and south cliffs at Redcliff's Beach. Remembering all this in nanoseconds, Beth stares out at the waves licking at the nearest perfectly sculpted sand dune and feels the softness touch on her cheek and she says, "Good morning, sweet Dandelion. Are you ready for our run?"

As an answer, the large orange cat leaps off the table and struts to the slider door and purrs loudly. Standing, Beth stretches as she says. "Okay, kiddo, I'm ready too. Let's go run."

Within minutes, Beth nears the red cliffs at the north end of the beach and passes the last perfectly sculpted sand dune next to the slab of granite, then thinks,

I was so lucky Tom Ames came that day of the storm. He and the cleanup crew cleared that mess of debris and logs by the end of the day. The beach flat and a mess of float logs. His skill with the digger/dozer brought this beach back to a beautiful life. Now the sea grass and the dunes have doubled in size even after withstanding several fierce storms this winter.

As she passes the sand dune, her cat suddenly rushes out from the dune's tall sea grass and tags her ankle before scampers under a float log the edge of the dune. Laughing, Beth steps onto the granite slab at the base of the north cliffs, then looks back for the cat. Not seeing Dandy anywhere, she calls out, "Dandelion? Come here. Dandy, come. Come stay beside me."

At the sound of her voice, the cat pokes out from her hidey hole within the debris and scampers across the sand with loud scolding cries. Once the animal is tucked between her feet and the cliff face, Beth leans her forehead on the stone and listens to whatever messages are there for her. While this is happening, the cat lies next to the cliff face and meticulously cleans itself, purring loudly.

The energy flow from the glowing touchstone is especially intense this morning and many images flood through Beth's mind. One image pushes it way into focus and shows the face of her niece, Nicole McGowan, within the glowing stone's protruding surface. Startled by a face she knows so well, Beth shouts, "What? Why is Nicole here? Are you sure this is meant for me?"

Then the image shows that Nicole is in a large room talking to a woman sitting at a reception desk. The woman stands and comes around to Nicole. Then the two women walk down a long hall, through two sets of locked doors and stop in front of a side door in the hallway. This door has a small door at eyelevel and the woman opens it to look inside. Then she lets Beth look through the small opening which has steel mesh across the opening. Once the small door is closed, the woman unlocks the full sized door it is in and opens it for both of them to walk inside.

When Nicole is in the room beyond, Beth sees how the room is furnished. There are comfortable looking chairs in front of the only window in the room. A single bed is to the left of these and a small table with one wooden chair is next to it. The bed is covered with fitted sheets, one blanket and one pillow.

Seated in front of the barred window, in the chair to the right, is a woman. She stares out the window and when the door opens, the woman turns to face the women coming into her room. Its then that Beth sees this other woman is Dee McGowan, her sister and Nicole's mother, known to officials as Dana Marie Anderson McGowan. Convicted a year ago of shooting to kill her sister, Beth Anderson and committed to the asylum for the criminally insane for a term of ten years or longer.

The image, within the golden touchstone, shows Nicole speaking to the woman. Then she crosses the room, kisses her mother's cheek and sits down in the other chair by the window. Taking her mother's hand in both of hers, Nicole talks to her mother for several minutes and Dee responds with smiling nods.

Suddenly, Dee pulls her hand away from Nicole's and shouts something which causes Nicole to stand and shake her head vigorously. Leaping upwards, Dee slaps her daughter's face very hard. Instantly, Nicole rushes to the door and pounds on it until a man in a white jacket opens it from the outside. Without talking to him, Nicole runs down the hallway through both pairs of doors and comes to the reception desk. The same woman stops Nicole and speaks with her for some time.

It's then that Beth sees two men in white coats rush past Nicole and the woman talking to her. The men go through the locked doors in the hallway and go into Dee's room. After a few minutes, the men come out of the hallway and wave to the women talking to Nicole at the desk.

Then the woman and Nicole go back to her mother's room. This time the image of Dee is very different than before. This time, Dee is wrapped into a white straightjacket with both her arms and hands pulled behind her back. She is seated in the same chair, in front of the barred window. However, her hair is messed and her face is filled with rage.

Nicole walks to stand behind the chair she'd sat in before and says something to her mother, keeping the chair between them. The young woman is crying as she speaks and Dee glares at her with hate filled eyes.

After several minutes, it seems the two begin to chat amiably and the woman, from the desk leaves the room. However, when the door clicks shut, Dee McGowan leaps from her chair and butts Nicole with her head. Undone by the attack, Nicole starts towards the door out of the room and Dee rams her head into Nicole's back, causing her daughter to trip and fall to the floor. Without a second between them,

Dee repeatedly kicks at her daughter's head and body. Trying to avoid the blows, Nicole rolls back and forth across the floor, all the while screaming for help.

Within seconds, the door flies open and four people in white coats rush into the room and yank Dee away from Nicole. Two of the people help Nicole onto her feet and check over the bruises on her head. The other men hold Dee down on her bed and lash her to it with leather straps attached to the bedframe. Nicole watches until this is done. Only when she is sure the restraints are secure Dee does Nicole turn away. It's then that the image fades.

Exhausted by the images, Beth sits down against the cliff face and puts her head in her hands for several minutes. Finally, Dandelion comes to her lap and purrs loudly. Pulling the animal into her arms, Beth buries her face in the warmth of the loving cat and she asks, "Why show that to me, Dandy, why to me? Was it a warning of things to come or did it already happened?"

Suddenly furious, Beth's shouts, "The damn bitch!", and the cat leaps from her arms, races past the sea grass topped dune and hides in the rip-rap next to the roundabout at the end of Shoreline Drive.

Still furious, Beth shakes her fist at the sky and shouts, "Damn you Dee McGowan. How could you be so brutal to your child? Nicole loves you so much. And, you, you damn touchstone, don't show me anymore about that damned sister or mine. I don't want to see how she treats her children. Dump that load of shit on their father's shoulders, not mine."

Turning to the glowing touchstone in the cliff face, Beth slaps it hard and screams, "I declare this run good and done."

In that instant, as if its tail is on fire, the orange cat streaks out from the rip-rap where it'd hid, races across the narrow slice of sand, flashes over the granite slab and leaps into Beth's arms. Surprised by the cat's actions, Beth catches the animal with both hands and laughs with delight. "Whoa, you crazy, crazy cat. What a joy you are, my friend. I'm so glad Nicole gave you to me last year and that you come with me on these runs. I really, really, really, needed you today. Let's slap the touchstone together, one more time. Then we'll go home."

Holding one of Dandy's front paws in her own hand, Beth taps the touchstone with it and says, "I declare this run good and done."

Then, to Beth's astonishment, the cat reaches out the same paw, taps the glowing stone three times and loudly meows. Cuddling the large cat, Beth tells it, "Dandy Dandelion, my darling kitty cat, I'm beginning to think you know more about this stone I do. Are you getting messages from it, too?"

Taking a deep breath, Beth exhales into the lush fur along the cat's back and hears the animal's deep purr. Rocking gently, Beth cradles it in her arms as if a small child and the negative energy from the vision spins off and out to the Universe. Feeling the release, Beth says, "Let's go home, Dandy. I'm tired being shown or told about things I have no control over."

Stepping off the granite slab, Beth sets Dandy on the sand and starts towards home. It's then that she hears a faint rumbling sound, coming from the south. Climbing to the top of the large sand dune near the cliffs, she shields her eyes from the sun and peers into the distance trying to see what is making the sound. Seeing nothing, yet noticing the sound continually gets louder, Beth waits, and, after a few minutes, she sees a long silver shape moving up from the south curve on Shoreline Drive.

Looking down at the cat sitting between her feet, Beth says, "Dandy, what the hell is that thing? It sounds like a big semi is coming this way. Maybe it's Tom Ames with his heavy equipment. No, it isn't him. That thing's too shiny to be any of Tom's rigs. It looks like…yes, by gosh, it is. It's a big diesel pickup towing a long silver trailer. Holy cow, Dandy, that rig's at least fifty feet long. And that has to be a new Airstream trailer, it's so shiny. Whoa… look at that rig tear up the road. Whoever's behind the wheel of that beast better start slowing down or they'll be up and over these cliffs before they know it."

Watching the long big rig roar past her cabin, Beth hears its gears begin to shift down. However, it's nearly at the roundabout at the end of Shoreline Drive, before the rig finally shows signs of slowing. Holding her breath, Beth knows the rig is still going too fast to stop and she watches wide-eyed as the diesel truck and long Airstream trailer goes into the roundabout for the first time, throwing gravel off the shoulder of the road as it makes the long bend.

With loud hissing and an arched back, Dandy leaps from Beth's arms, hides in the tall sea grass at Beth's feet and growls loudly at the rig slowly slowing on the roundabout. Finally on its fourth round, the rig shifts low enough and comes to a full stop at the sheltered high point on Shoreline Drive, in front of the only path up to the cliffs.

For several seconds, Beth waits at the edge of the roundabout for someone to emerge from the cab on the pickup. Then, as answering her unspoken question, the cab door swings open with a jolt and, when no one comes out, she calls out, "Hello? You in the truck? Is anybody there or did the truck drive itself up here?"

Instantly, a dark haired woman pops her head into view and smiles as she steps onto the running board below the cab's door. Waving to Beth, she asks, "You wouldn't happen to be Beth Anderson, would you?"

"I certainly would be. Are you that bronco truck taming rodeo queen known as Dr. Lucy Wong?"

Laughing, the woman hops down to the pavement and strides over to Beth with one hand extended for a handshake. Quickly noting the woman's petite size, lovely golden skin and thick black hair glistening in the morning sun, Beth reaches out her own hand and the women shake hands. Then the short woman pulls Beth into a hug and at this time both note their extreme height difference.

Laughing with delighted surprise, Beth grins down at the petite woman and says, "Maybe we should just call each other Mutt and Jeff. However, if you think I'm tall, you should see my sister. Then again, hopefully, you won't meet her as she's locked up for years in an asylum for the criminally insane."

"What can I say? My folks are short and Chinese and I have their genetics. However, that's the not the only thing I can blame on them. All the other stuff, you'll learn about in the next year. But right now, I'll apologize for my obsessive compulsive behavior before we go any further."

Enjoying the banter, Beth laughs heartily and says, "Welcome to

Redcliff's Beach, Dr. Wong. I'm so happy that the survey for the Maxine Oakley Preserve is getting started. I received your letter of introduction last week and, before that, I got one from the State Department of Fisheries and Wildlife. They had some pretty fine things to say about you."

"That's good to hear. But, please, Beth, call me Lucy. I want to thank you for being here to greet me. I sure didn't expect a welcoming committee." As she speaks, Lucy makes a sweeping motion towards the trailer and says, "Do you like my new home? It's my abode, laboratory and visitor center all wrapped into this one wonderful Airstream. It's the Department of F&W donation to the effort and holds all I need for the next five years."

"It's wonderful, Lucy. I'm impressed. For a while, though, I thought it was going to take you up that dirt road and over the top of the cliffs. Glad you got that beast of a truck under control."

Laughing at Beth's observation, Lucy says, "I admit that I was a bit concerned, too. If I'd crashed on my first day here, I doubt I'd get any more funds from the State to do the sea life survey on the Maxine Oakley Preserve. I hope I'm successful and that you and I become great friends. It's so nice to finally meet you, Beth."

"I'll say the same, Lucy. I'm also glad they sent a woman to do the study on the preserve instead of some burly man. It's going to be great having you as a neighbor."

"I'm so pleased that you're pleased. I was concerned that you'd feel slighted when you saw me instead of one of the big bulls. Some people still regard women as second stringers for any position. It's very nice to hear you don't. I see you brought a welcoming committee with you"

Turning to where Lucy points, Beth laughs, "That big bad cat is Dandy, short for Dandelion. She thinks she's a Cheetah in disguise. I should rename her Cheeky as she always plays the part. Come here, Dandelion. Meet Dr. Lucy Wong. She's our new neighbor."

Instantly, the large cat pops out from between two boulders at the side of the roundabout and struts towards the two women with her tail raised high over her back. Without hesitation, the animal goes directly to Lucy and rubs back and forth across the woman's shins. Chuckling, Lucy Wong bends to run her fingers through the animal's thick fur and says, "Hello to you too, Dandelion. Good to meet you."

Beth exclaims, "I am impressed, Lucy. Dandy usually hides for at least an hour before coming out when anyone new appears. She must feel as I do, that you're perfect for Redcliff's Beach and the Maxine Oakley Preserve."

Smiling with pleasure, Lucy replies, "Your being here, Beth, gives me a chance to tell you how wonderful it was that you turned your land over to the State to be held as a preserve. It will be at least two years before the preserve is fully ready to open to the public. I've heard so much about you and Maxine from your associates at the University. You both have terrific reputations on campus. Is it true you were together for over thirty years?"

"Yes. Thirty amazingly wonderful years." Beth says, beaming at the young face in front of her.

"I first heard about the preserve late last summer and the announcement simply said a species survey was to be done on the tide flats. I decided to apply for the position even though I was still in grad-school. I figured that by the time they got around to requesting resumes, I'd have my Doctorate in Biology and Botany and be well on my way to a Doctorate in Oceanography. I'm overqualified but those degrees got me the job."

Nodding, Beth adds, "I don't think a woman can have too much education. Maxine and I met while working on our doctorates. Over the years, we found having those letters behind our names put us ahead of many others applying for the same upgrades or positions at the University."

"Yes, I agree, the years of cramming night after night are worth it. However, I hadn't factored in the need for funding. After I was offered the position, the Department of Fish and Wildlife began dragging their feet and I prodded the department head as to what the holdup was. When he told me it was a matter of funding. I told him I would cover my own expenses if they would give me publication rights of my survey results as it's that publication that will finalize my Doctorate in

Oceanography. Almost overnight, the Department head found funds for the truck and trailer along with some funding for supplies. Eventually, there'll be buildings at both ends of the beach. This end will have the office and staff residences. The south end will have the visitor facilities."

"Well, it's great to have you here, Lucy. I was beginning to think the State had forgotten all about the preserve until I got their letter announcing your appointment. Is there anything I can do to help? If so, just give a shout out."

"How about right now? I could sure use an extra body to help unhook and stabilize my trailer. The setup takes one person a half day but two can do it in just over an hour."

"Sure thing, Dandy and I would love to do anything we can to get you settled and the beach survey going. Could Dandy watch from inside your truck? It's pretty open on the roundabout and I see the bald eagles are beginning to circle overhead."

Once Dandy is safely inside the truck's cab, Beth and Lucy unhook, level and stabilize the trailer. When that's done, Beth extends the a green and white striped awning attached to the top of the trailer while Lucy pulls out and sets up two long tables and unfolds a couple of beach chairs. When this is done, Lucy says, "Okay, Beth. Time for a break. How does a tall glass of lemonade and cookies sound?"

"Great! Could I get a bowl of fresh water for Dandy?"

Minutes later the two women are chatting under the awning, sipping cold drinks as Dandy laps from a small bowl placed under Beth's chair. When the cat finishes, it leaps onto Beth's lap and settles down for a nap as the women chatter over her.

An hour later, Beth stands, still holding Dandy in her arms, and says, "It's time I get out of here so you can finish getting settled. If you don't have other plans, why don't you come down for dinner tonight? I'll give you a rough history of the beach, as I know it. Afterwards, we'll watch the sunset over glasses of wine. If you want to walk down. I'll be glad to drive you home."

"That sounds great, Beth, I need to stretch my legs after that long drive. Dinner sounds perfect. Thanks so much." Lucy responds happily.

"Just one more thing. Move your truck from the front of your trailer. Where it is now blocks the one path up to the cliffs and the locals use it daily with more coming on weekends. They see the cliff tops the best place for picnics, watching whales and sunsets." Beth warns her new neighbor.

"Thanks for the tip. Eventually, that track will be closed to unofficial traffic as the residential buildings will go up there. We'll probably have to carve a trail through those woods so people can get to the beaches to the north. What time should I come tonight?"

"Five or whenever you get your work done. We'll chat over glasses of iced tea or wine, fresh baked bread and salads. Is steak okay with you? Great. See you later. Come on, Dandy. It's time to get home." That said, Beth jogs down the road with the cat running through the tall weeds growing along the edge of the road.

During their dinner of grilled steaks and salad greens, Beth and Lucy share their life stories. After the dishes are washed and put away, the two woman refill their glasses and take the wine out to the deck chairs to toast the glorious sunset. By that time, both are feeling they've found a new friend. Totally at ease with each other, Lucy asks to hear about the cabin and how it came to be built.

For the next hour, Beth tells how her father, James Anderson, built the cabin for his family, his wife Jill and his two daughters Dana Marie and Elizabeth Ann. The she explains why she and Maxine came to live full time at the cabin. As she tells of the decision to give the land to the State of Washington and naming it the Maxine Oakley Preserve.

Happy to share everything, Beth tells of adding the north wing and ends her explanation by saying "After that terrible storm last year, I had Tom Ames put on the garage doors and cover the south side deck to the original entry. The enclosed garage is a great place to work, even during the worst months."

Lucy says, "I've heard about those winter storms. That's why I had the awning added to the outside of the trailer. That storm last year must have been a doozy. I'm hoping the State will put up a building before too many winters go by. It's my only request and I'm going to nag them until it's built. If that notorious Pineapple Express hits as it has in the past, I may retreat down here and stay with you."

"You're more than welcome to do so. However, I'm not sure if this is the best place to be when one of those hits the beach." Beth tells her, "I went through hell with that one last year. You keep nagging the State for your building on the cliff tops. Until then, you can store anything you want in one of the cabinets out in the garage. That area was the one place not totally washed away by the storm that trashed most of the cabin."

"Thank you so much, I was going to ask if I could attach one insulated steel cabinet to that empty spot along the south wall in your garage. It would really open up some much needed space in my rig. I'd use it to store dry supplies and dehydrated specimens."

"Sure, bring it down any time you want. Sounds heavy so give me a shout and I'll help you with it. Sooner is better than later, then you'll can set up your equipment as you want it in your rig. There's a refrigerator out there I don't use anymore and you're welcome to use it."

"Thanks, I just might take you up on that. I'd planned to keep fresh samples in my own fridge, but during the winter months that fridge would let me store several digs and do the tests when the weather is impossible to get out. I thought I'd dump any leftovers on the beach for the gulls to cleanup."

"Oh boy, are those birds ever going to love you. Just don't let them follow you back to the trailer or they'll be sitting out there waiting for you. Believe me, seagulls can become royal pests. Save a week's samples, then drive it down to the south and toss it off the cliffs. No matter what you do, they'll eventually figure out where you're coming from. Those damn birds are so smart."

As the women talk, the sunset spreads its brilliant colors across the horizon and the two fall silent until the afterglow vanishes. When stars dance brightly overhead, Lucy stands and announces, "Time for me to call it a day."

Setting their wine glasses in the kitchen sink, Beth pulls two flashlights from a drawer and says, "You've had a long day, Lucy, so it's your choice. We can take a walk to the north cliffs and slap my touchstone or I can drive you home in five minutes. Your pleasure."

"I'd love the beach walk. It's such a beautiful night. I haven't seen stars like these in years. We city folk don't know what we miss surrounded by lights all night."

As they trek up the beach, Lucy shines her light on the beach and over the high sea-grass topped dunes. Finally, she points the flashlight at the highest dune and moves the light over the tall sea-grass covering its top. "I'm really amazed at how perfect these dunes are. It's as if someone decided to put them in the exact place they were needed and then pushed them into these wonderful shapes. The sand dunes I've seen on other beaches have been moved around by wind and waves into much different shapes.

"It's going to be interesting to see how the wind and tides shaped these so perfectly. The dunes south of your cabin are more like those I've seen on other beaches. Look, over there, see what I mean? That dune's grass has a tended look. It's as if it's been planted to grow in those lovely groupings. It's truly something I've never seen before and it fascinates me."

Listening without comment, Beth decides to tell Lucy the truth about the dunes. Clearing her throat and touches Lucy's arm. "Lucy? Stop here for a few minutes, I need to tell you something. After I've told you, you can do whatever your conscience tells you to do. However, I must emphasis that at the time it was done, it seemed the best thing to do. Remember what I told you about the storm that hit this beach last year? In a week it will be exactly one year ago."

With that said, Beth bares her heart to Lucy and retells the story of the perfect storm which tore through her cabin. Then, she tells how a community of people came out to make everything right for her again. "Nobody can tell me those people weren't angels, Lucy. In less than a week, the cabin was completely redone, yet is still the one my father built.

"The real angel that came that day was a man called Tom Ames. He owns a local landscaping business and brought out his digger/dozer. It was this machine that lifted those huge logs from inside the cabin. Later, he used the same logs for bulkheads around the cabin and sand dunes around others. His whole purpose was to make the cabin and north beach safe for years to come.

"When he was done down there, he planted drift logs up to the north cliffs and sculpted these wonderful dunes. I bought and planted fifty flats of sea-grass on top of these same dunes. The two of us worked as a team and when we were finished this beach was more beautiful than it had been for decades. Last winter, these dunes held back three storms from causing more erosion along the shoreline and around my cabin. You can see for yourself that they are doing exactly what we'd hoped they would. Each of these dunes is twice their original size and the grasses have become the lush growths you noticed.

"As I said, I'm not going to tell you what to do with this information. I like you very much and will respect whatever decision you make. I've told you this as I decided that whatever friendship is developing between the two of us has to be based on honesty. I ask only that you study the results before you take any action and to remember that I was as involved in the decision as Tom Ames was."

For several minutes, Lucy silently moves her flashlight over the near dunes. Then she says, "They look as if Tom knew exactly what to do. As I said, it's amazing how the dunes seem so tied into place. However, I wonder why you didn't apply for the needed permits to do the work."

Beth replies, "We just didn't, Lucy. First off, I didn't think of it as I was too busy trying to reclaim my life. I'm sure Tom didn't as it's been said that any fine 'after the fact' is small compared to the fees and time it takes to get proper permitting to do any work along waterfront now days. People who do it the 'right way' jump through hoops for years. The feeling of those who live on waterfront property is that it's better to get your hands slapped for having done naughty than to deal with bureaucracy for months and years before anything can happen."

Lucy shines her light over the dunes and then to the granite slab at the base of the north cliffs and says, "Hey, girlfriend, weren't you going to show me how to slap your touchstone?" Then, with a whoop of laughter, she begins to run towards the north cliffs.

Taken by surprise, Beth shouts, "Hey, you stinker. Wait for me. It's my touchstone."

THREE

June 1ˢᵗ—Eliza

ELIZA runs at the edge of the waves trying to avoid the crowds of people flying kites, throwing Frisbees, splashing in and out of the incoming waves or on their own runs. Approaching a group watching a dead seal being stripped into pieces by two adult bald eagles and a juvenile along with a flock of seagulls and a murder of crows picking up whatever the eagles discard. Disgusted by the crowd's interest, Eliza shouts, "Let the birds do their work, you damned idiots."

Ignoring snide responses to her jibe, Eliza has passed the group and is heading to the north cliffs, when she hears her name shouted. Turning, she sees her neighbors, Al and Penny, running towards her and away from the dead seal. When the couple reaches her, Penny says, "We came out early to watch the sunrise. The colors were just beautiful but I'm afraid that means a storm's coming our way. Isn't that what the poem 'red in the morning, better take warning' means?"

Her husband laughs and says, "Maybe so, silly, but that sunrise was worth whatever storm is coming, wasn't it? If the weather turns bad before our bonfire tonight we'll just move the gang into our house. That's why I stopped you, Eliza. You're coming tonight, aren't you?"

"No, not this time, Al. I told Penny yesterday that I'm picking up Marie and her twins at the Portland Airport late this afternoon. The twins just graduated from the University of Colorado and Marie's bringing them home for the summer. She went last month to enjoy all the celebrations on campus and at the girls' sorority. It sounds as if they had a great time. It'll be good to have her back home and hear about it all. Small as my house is, it's pretty empty without Marie's chatter. Put me on the list to host a picnic, Penny. Marie and I love these neighborhood gatherings you and Al started last summer. They help all of us year round residents feel as if we're a real community. Just tell us the date, okay?" Moving away as she says these last words, Eliza waves and shouts over her shoulder, "Have fun. We'll see you soon."

Picking up her pace, Eliza runs with a steady beat, waving to people only if they wave first. When she steps onto the huge granite slab at the base of the north cliffs, she looks back at the beach and sees that mist is rising off the sun heated tide flats. Even as she watches, the mist becomes a fog so thick that people on the beach drop in and out of sight.

Turning to the large glowing stone in the cliff face, she slaps it hard and shouts, "I declare this run good and done." Instantly a large crack opens beside the touchstone splitting the granite cliff face with a loud snapping noise. Startled, Eliza jumps off to the far side and stares at the opening as it becomes a high arched entrance into a cave. When nothing more changes to the opening, Eliza steps up to the wide entrance and sees a long tunnel that goes through the cliffs to a beach of golden sand at the far end.

Sunlight, coming through the opening, lights the tunnel enough for Eliza to see there is a well-used path to the far end. Excited by this surprising find, she starts to move into the tunnel's entrance, but stops when she hears a deep grinding sound. Backing away, she sees that the translucent touchstone is moving out from the cliff face. Its length grows until it drops to the edge of the granite slab and slides off to bury its tip into the rocky beach below. As she watches, steps appear to be cut into the full length of the long stone creating a twelve foot ladder that leans against the, now, ten foot high granite slab.

Finally seeing a way down from the stone she is standing upon, Eliza moves towards the ladder. Then stops and stares around her, finally realizing all the changes that have happened. "Where's my Redcliff's Beach? This isn't it."

Unsure of what to do, Eliza goes back to stand next to the opening of the tunnel and sees it is very dark inside as if the other end has completely closed. Then she hears a woman's voice singing a song that Eliza feels she knows and looks in the direction of the voice. Walking to the stone ladder, she expects to see the person stepping onto the granite slab. When no one is there, she moves to the edge of the slab and looks down at the bottom of the stone steps.

On the rocky beach, ten feet below, a woman with short white hair looks up at her. Delighted by the woman's smile and appearance, Eliza watches the woman start up the stone ladder. Hurrying over to stand where she can greet the woman as soon as she steps onto the granite slab, Eliza has no doubts that this woman is another Parallel Life of the original child named Elizabeth Ann Anderson. Just as she is.

When this new Elizabeth Ann climbs to the top of the ladder and steps onto the granite slab, the woman turns back to the top of the touchstone stairs, slaps the top of it and shouts, "I declare this run is good and done."

Spreading her arms wide open, Eliza shouts, "Hello Elizabeth Ann, I'm so glad to meet you there."

The smiling woman looks at Eliza and walks directly up to her, then passes through her without missing a step. Feeling nothing of the woman as she passes through her, Eliza turns and watches the woman enter the opening into the long tunnel and disappear. Totally stunned at the woman's body passing through her own body without feeling one thing, Eliza runs to the opening and sees a dark shape running out the far end onto a beach of golden sand.

Eliza shouts, "Nothing, there was nothing to you but air. Not one damned thing. There wasn't a wisp of air or a puff of scent. Nothing. When I wrapped my arms around you, there was nothing. Nothing. Who are you? Hell, what are you? Were you just my imagination?"

Her answer comes as a loud grinding sound which causes Eliza to turn and see the touchstone moving back into the cliff face. Watching the touchstone reset itself into the cliff face and cave entrance close, Beth also sees that Redcliff's Beach is again as she has always known it to be and a mile to the south, the greenish gleam of the aged copper beacons her home.

Leaping onto the sandy beach, Eliza runs at the edge of the incoming waves without noticing anyone or anything. All her thoughts are on the woman who sang the song and walked right through her body.

Late that afternoon, Eliza has changed into her city clothes and, checking her Smartphone for any calls or texts she may have missed from Marie before her plane took off, she finds there are three. Smiling, she opens the messages and listens to them with a wide smile she hears the excitement in Marie's and the twins' voices as they talk about getting home to Redcliff's Beach. When she has listened to them each three times, Eliza sends each of the messages to 'SAVE' and turns off the phone.

Knowing the plane is due to land at the Portland International Airport in four hours, she collects her purse and keys and goes down to the main room. Going into the kitchen to get a glass of iced tea, she takes it to the dining table and thinks about having the twins here all summer.

"It'll be so lovely watching Julia and Janice see their new suites for the first time. Placing them under the front deck was such a great idea. The twins can feel independent yet close enough for Marie to keep in on their plans for each day. For once, I'll be in on their plans before they happen and possibly have a helpful bit of advice for their futures. If nothing else, it's going to be a summer to remember for years and years." Eliza chuckles at the possibilities.

Taking her empty glass to the dishwasher, Eliza hears a cat's meow and sees Beth's cat, Dandelion, curled up on the golden stone under the dining table. "Hey, Dandy, what are you doing here without Beth?"

The cat looks at her with bright golden eyes, stretches, then walks over to be picked up. Cuddling the large cat in her arms, Eliza feels a pang which childless women often feel when the time is long past. Taking Dandy to her chair, she sits at the moment Beth appears at her end of the adjoined tables.

Seeing Eliza's bundle, Beth laughs and says, "Hey gal, I see Dandy's got you tied around her little finger, or should that be a claw? Anyway, how is everything going for you?"

Eliza replies, "Hey yourself, kiddo. Dandy just wanted to say Hi before I take off for the Portland Airport to pick up Marie and the twins. Would she go on a car ride? I'd have her back by midnight."

Beth laughs and says, "Maybe you better not. No telling when she might turn into the cheetah she thinks she is."

Laughing, Eliza sets the cat on the floor and moves around the tables to give Beth a hug. At the same time, Dandy curls around the golden stone under the table and begins to purr loudly.

"Beth, do you have time to hear what happened at the cliffs this morning?"

"Sure and I need to update you on info the touchstones gave us earlier this week. You first, though."

"I went late to the cliffs this morning. No excuses, just felt lazy. Right after I slapped the touchstone, there was a snapping sound and my dimension changed into another dimension...." And for the next several minutes Eliza describes her experiences at the touchstone.

Listening to her adventure, Beth jots notes and when Eliza finishes, Beth says, "I'm so glad you didn't go too far into that cave. You're the first one to have such an experience. The touchstone says to be cautious about going into unknown dimensions. It also wants each of us to ask the touchstone for information it has before you slap it. You're to put your forehead to the stone and ask if there are messages for you. After it tells you what you are to know, then you can slap the touchstone and shout your mantra. Liz talks to it every day, as I do. You should do it, too. Especially now that you've gone into another dimensions."

A smile crosses Eliza's face as she says, "I didn't feel any real danger, Beth. Besides, would we be shown these things if they were dangerous to us. Honestly, if the woman had seen me and stopped to talk to me, I would have gone with her into the cave and out the other end. I'm sure I would have returned to this dimension sometime within this same day. I'm not going to be frightened whenever I encounter something new and unusual. This adventure called the Parallel Lives of Elizabeth Ann is too wonderful to hold back on anything. We should grab onto each new thing shown to us and discover whatever it's come to teach us."

Beth looks at Eliza with a new appreciation and says, "Wow, what a great way to look at these experiences that pop into our lives, Eliza. You are so right. We should do whatever our hearts tell us to do at the time. That way, if a new dimension or a new Elizabeth Ann comes into our lives, we can feel free to learn as much as possible about them. You've made me realize that I'm too cautious about interrupting what the touchstone tells me. I think it's time for me to change the way I approach new events that come into my life."

Eliza smiles at Beth's compliment and says, "Thanks, Beth. I like knowing you have a positive attitude about me. I've loved having you and Liz in my life. What was it that you were you going to tell me?"

"I've a new neighbor parked on the roundabout at the end of Shoreline Drive. Her name is Dr. Lucy Wong and she's been hired to do the survey on the Maxine Oakley Preserve...."

After Beth tells Eliza all she knows about Lucy, she adds, "Lucy's coming for dinner tonight, maybe you'll see her then."

Shaking her head, Eliza says, "Not today. I'm leaving right now to go pick up Marie and her daughters at the Portland Airport. We won't be back till late. I'll look for Lucy some other time. Welcome her for me, I'll see you tomorrow for sure."

Eliza's drive to Portland goes smoothly and, by five that afternoon, she turns into the departure lanes of Portland International Airport. Letting her BMW slow to a crawl, she eases the car past lines of parked taxis and vans until she sees the gate number where Marie said she and the twins would wait. As she moves the car forward, a space suddenly opens and she flips on her right turn signal. Tapping her brakes several times to let the passenger van following her know that she is going to stop, she moves the car into the open space and slows to a stop.

After shifting the car into park, she reaches to unlock her seatbelt and, in that instant, the rear of her car is rammed by the passenger van. The hard jolt tosses Eliza forward and, though the seatbelt keeps her shoulders tight to the back of the seat, the front airbags don't open and her forehead taps the steering wheel.

Rubbing the smarting spot, Eliza looks in the rearview mirror and sees the van's driver jump out of his vehicle, check his front bumper, swear at the damage and, instead of checking to see if Eliza is injured, the man rushes through the doors into the Airport and disappears. Shaking from the hard jolt, Eliza stays in her car listening to loud speakers blare warnings of not leaving cars unattended. Looking around the area, she also sees three signs blinking the same message.

Finally, she gets out and moves to the rear of her car. As she is checking the rear bumper for damage, a patrol car with its lights flashing pulls alongside. When the officer gets out, she asks, "Any damage done?"

"None that I see on the rear of my car, no thanks to that driver. However, the van's bumper and license plate are totally smashed. I'm taking down his license number for my insurance agent in case there's any damage to my car's internal system. I'd already stopped, turned the engine off and shifted into park. What a jerk that guy was. The asshole didn't even check to see if anyone in my car was hurt. Just rammed me, jumped out, and ran into the airport. I'm glad you're going to give him a ticket. You are, aren't you?"

"Oh, yes. He's getting a ticket. Not for ramming your car, as I don't see any damage to it. The ticket is for leaving his vehicle unattended and leaving the scene of an accident. For that, he'll get a big fine. We have to give tickets every time a car is left unattended or no one would believe the signs or loudspeakers. The fines start at five hundred and go up. This one is definitely a 'way up'. Are you waiting for someone?"

"Yes, my sister and nieces. I always pick them up in Departures.

They should be here very soon." Eliza points at the doors Marie and the twins would come out. "Their plane landed a half-hour ago. How long can I sit here?"

Looking at the officer, Eliza sees the woman is listening to her car radio. When she turns back to Eliza, she asks, "Which flight did you say they were to come in on?"

"Delta 255." Eliza tells her.

Again, the woman opens the car door to respond to the car's radio and speaks so low that Eliza watches passively. However, when the officer exclaims loudly and looks her way giving a nod to her receiver, Eliza's stomach muscles tighten. Then the officer hangs the receiver back on its hook and Eliza turns away to look at the doors where her sister should soon be coming out from building. As the officer walks up beside her, Eliza holds her breath against what she is certain she is going to hear.

"Ma'am? I checked with the airline and it seems there was a problem with the plane with that flight number. It's been delayed for some time. The airline has opened a room at the Hyatt across the way and I'm to lead you over there. Get in your car and pull in front of mine. When we are moving, I'll hit the siren, pass you and lead you to the hotel. There's reserved parking for these sorts of incidents. The parking is free and you'll be able to wait for your sister's flight in comfort. They'll know over there what the plane's final eta is."

Without waiting for her answer, the patrolwoman gets into the patrol car and starts the motor. When she sees Eliza hasn't moved from the rear of her car, the officer opens the side window and yells for Eliza to move her car out in front. Hearing the sharpness in the officer's voice, Eliza does as told and soon the BMW is following the patrol car through and out of the airport traffic. Staying close to the patrol car, Eliza follows it into the Hyatt's parking area.

Stopping beside the patrol car, she feels sobs begin deep inside. No one can tell her this is normal procedure for late arriving planes. No, no, no, no, she wants to scream but her throat is too dry and the words can't escape. Then a voice scolds,

Stop it, Eliza. Get hold of yourself. Do it for me, for us. Do you hear me?

It's then that Eliza becomes the stoic businesswoman she'd always been running Staples Fruit Packing Company for thirty years. Getting out of her car, she follows the patrolwoman into the hotel lobby and sees the faces of the hotel staff as they look her way. She knows to be ready for the most shocking of tragedies and, more than anything else at that moment, Eliza wants Marie and the twins to be proud of her. Again the voice speaks to her,

No screaming. No fainting. You are Eliza Staples.

Leading her to and through a double door, the officer goes to a woman at a desk and whispers something. Immediately, the woman springs from behind the desk and thanks the officer who disappears without a word to Eliza. The woman then leads Eliza into an area where several sofas and chairs are filled with people huddling in forlorn groups. From the looks on their faces, Eliza knows their lives have changed radically and she knows hers is about to do the same.

Her unspoken question is answered when the woman asks, "Could you tell me how many of your loved ones were on the flight, Delta 255?"

Seeing Eliza's stunned look, the woman continues, "Please, come sit on the sofa and tell me their names. I need their information and where we can reach you after you leave here. You understand that flight is not going to land here at Portland, don't you?"

"No, I don't understand that. Tell me what has happened. Why doesn't someone just tell me what happened? Why do you want this information about me and my family? Why haven't you told me what happened? Has the plane crashed? How? When? Please. Tell me now." Eliza shouts her last words causing all the heads in the room to turn and stare at her with sad, hopeless, faces.

The woman immediately holds Eliza's around the shoulders and leads her to a sofa where one small boy sits. When the woman settles next to the child, the boy scurries over to his family and the woman pulls Eliza down beside her, saying, "Please, forgive my stupidity. I assumed the officer told you that Delta 255 had crashed after takeoff. It happened over three hours ago. I'm so sorry that the patrolperson didn't tell you that information before you got here.

"The worst part is that we know for certain there are no survivors. All those on board were killed immediately on impact. There are no survivors, none. I'm so very sorry to have to tell you this."

Eliza sighs a deep shuddering sigh and says, "I knew it. I felt it all the way to the airport, ever since I left home. I can't stay here. I must go home. I must get out of here and go home." She whispers, "Marie and the twins are waiting for me there. I know they are. I know it."

When she stands to go, the woman holds her hand and asks, "Could you stay long enough to fill out the form? We need their names and your phone number to make certain everyone is accounted for and that their families or friends have been contacted."

Eliza nods and follows the woman over to a desk, sits in the chair beside it and silently fills out the form with as much information she can remember. When finished, she stands, hands the form to the woman and says, "You can call me at this number if you need more information. Marie always takes out insurance with the twins as beneficiaries. Right now, I really need to use a restroom. Is there a toilet in here somewhere?"

The woman nods, points to a door with the word Women on it and says, "Over there. Then come back to me before you leave. I'll have a large coffee for you to take with you. Don't go without it nor the cookies I'll put in a sack for you. Both will help get you home safely."

When Eliza comes back to the woman, she takes the container of coffee and bag of cookies, then says, "Thank you for your kindness. This coffee will get me home. Bless you for being here for all of us."

Once back in her car, Eliza follows the signs onto I-205 and stays in the right hand lane as she crosses the Columbia River Bridge. Keeping just below the speed limit, she sees the exit turnoff into Fort Vancouver and drives down to Riverside Drive where her favorite restaurant sits on the north shore of the river. This was the restaurant where she planned a celebration for the twins' graduation from the University of Colorado and for Marie's return to Redcliff's Beach after being away for a month.

By the time she parks the car near the front entrance to the restaurant, Eliza is completely numb. Even so, she walks through the front door and, before the hostess can greet her, she tells the woman to cancel her dinner reservations. As she turns to go back out the door, the owner sees her and looks behind her for her sister and the twins, "Welcome Eliza. We've got your favorite table ready for you. Didn't your sister get back as planned?"

Looking at the man, Eliza whispers, "No, my friend, their plane crashed on takeoff. All the passengers were killed. I'm sorry but I've cancelled my reservations for tonight. I'll call you again."

At that, Eliza walks out the door, goes to her car, starts the engine and drives back up Riverside Drive to the freeway. The miles to the wild beaches along Washington's Pacific coast go by without her noticing. When the sign for the exit shows over her lane, Eliza turns onto it keeping under the fifty miles per hour speed limit as the road is narrow and winding.

At Aberdeen's city limits, the highway divides, but the speed drops to forty mph and she carefully follows the familiar lanes through the town's stoplights. Finally, she crosses the bridge into Hoquiam and comes to the five way stop light with roads leading to every direction. As the light is red, she picks up the container of coffee from the cup holder and sips the hot drink. The coffee's bittersweet taste is exactly what she needs. By the time the light turns green, the hot liquid has smoothed some of the exhaustion from her face.

Taking the sharp left turn onto the street leading out to the north beaches, she relaxes a bit as she knows she'll soon be back home at Redcliff's Beach. As she follows the line of tail lights ahead of her, Eliza concentrates of driving and pushes all thoughts of Marie or the twins into the deepest corner of her mind. Terrified that those thoughts will get loose, she knows she is too heartsick to fight them off.

Driving along Discovery Bay, she notices oncoming cars are flashing their headlights at her. Confused by this, she pulls into a turnoff and goes out to the front of the BMW to check on what they see which she doesn't know. Instantly, she sees that only the parking lights are turned on and, for some reason, this makes Eliza giggle. Soon, she is laughing so hard that she begins to wet her underpants. For some reason, the warmth of the urine running down her legs comforts her and makes her feel alive. The feel of the wetness coming from her own body seems to bring her back to life and makes her so happy that she lets the hot liquid soak her slacks and fill her loafers.

When she goes to the open car door and starts to get in the car, she hears her shoes squish. Unlatching the trunk, she goes to the rear of the car, opens the car's trunk and takes out an old woolen blanket she keeps there for emergencies. Then, still laughing, Eliza returns to the open door and covers the driver's seat before she sits behind the steering wheel and leans back in the comfort of the bucket seat. Taking up the paper coffee cup, Eliza drinks the last of the dark hot brew and eats all five of the frosted sugar cookies from the bag. When the last bite is gone, she crumbles the empty bag and stuffs it in the coffee container. Then, she tosses the container over her shoulder onto the back seat.

It is the toss of the container that brings the images of Marie and the twins, Julia and Janice, out from the corner of her mind and she cries out, "Oh my darlings, I love you so much. You are my family. Why were you taken? Why did you die? Is this horrible loss the payment for my sins? Were you the price I had to pay for killing Jack and Peg?"

Putting her head in her hands, Eliza screams, then pounds on the steering wheel with both her fists. When her anger so overwhelms her, she begins to punch at her face with her fists. Over and over, her blows pound at her head and feel so terrible that her blows to her head cause her ears to ring. Only when the inside of her car is filled with red and blue flashing light, does Eliza stop her flagellation and look into the rearview mirror and see a State Patrol Cruiser has pulled directly behind her car.

When the patrolman gets out and walks up to her side window, Eliza opens the door a crack and says, "I'm alright, officer. It's just that I lost my family in a plane crash today. Everyone aboard was killed and I just had to stop and cry. But I'm alright now. Really I am."

The patrolman opens the car door wider and bends down to say, "Please, ma'am, stay in your car. Open the window on this side and close the door."

"I was going to do that, but I have to start the car to do it and I didn't want you to think I was going to drive away." Eliza tells the man as she turns the key in the ignition. When the window is down, the patrolman closes the door and asks again if she is alright.

"Did I do something wrong? I only stopped to cry and drink my coffee. Do you want to see my license?"

"No, you're fine. We got a report of a woman screaming and hitting herself but I guess if your family died in a plane crash, you have a good reason to do that. I think I'd scream and beat myself if I ever lost my family. Do you want me to escort you home?"

"No, that's not necessary. I live at Redcliff's Beach. It's just up the road twenty or so miles. I'll drive carefully. Now that I've had my coffee and a good cry, I should be fine, just fine. Thank you anyway. You have a goodnight."

Giving a wave of her hand, Eliza pulls onto the highway behind a line of cars and follows them up past Ocean Shores. As she follows them, the cars peel off, one by one, in other directions, up driveways or turning onto intersecting roads. For the last five miles, Eliza's is the only car on the road. No cars follow her and only two pass her going the opposite direction... The night is dark and the once familiar road feels strange to her. Trying to shake off the eerie feeling, she turns on the radio to a classical station and turns the volume up loud.

Determined to get home before she has another breakdown, Eliza grips the steering wheel and guides the car around the familiar curves. When the last stretch of straight road shines in her headlights, she sees a flash of white and slows the car to a crawl. It's then that a large white dog runs into the middle of the road and stands facing her. As her car moves up to it, she honks the car horn and flashes the headlights trying to scare it off the road.

When it doesn't move and her car is a few feet from it, Eliza shouts out the window, "Shoo, dog, can't you see I'm coming at you?"

Instead of running off, the white dog trots to the front bumper and looks through the windshield at Eliza. Opening the car door, she steps out and claps her hands, shouting, "Go home. Shoo. Get out of here. Shoo."

When the dog still doesn't move, Eliza gets back in the car and carefully turns onto the shoulder and slowly passes the mysterious animal. Looking into the rearview mirror, she sees the dog is running after the car. Suddenly it races ahead of her and stops at the entrance into her driveway. Slamming on the brakes, Beth expects to hear a thump telling that she's hit the animal.

Instead, at the last second, the animal leaps over the top of her car and disappears into the night. Looking out the open car window, Eliza sees nothing behind her except headlights of a car coming up Shoreline Drive. Relieved, she rolls up the window and drives down to the garage door on her house as fast as she's ever driven the driveway. Only when the car is parked safely inside the garage and the garage door has rolled down behind it, does Eliza get out and rush through the door into her house.

Slamming and locking the door behind her, she runs up the stairs and goes into Marie's bedroom. Throwing herself on her sister's bed, Eliza lets loose the emotions she'd held back since hearing of the loss of her sister and nieces. Sobbing until she's exhausted, sleep finally finds her in Marie's bed, surrounded by the many remnants of Marie's life.

FOUR

June 5ᵗʰ—Liz

LIZ sees Kip watching her as she stands in front of the touchstone in the north cliffs and smiles at the dog, saying, "I thought we'd try to see the cave Eliza said she saw last week. I won't go inside as I take what the touchstones told us about not going into strange dimensions very seriously. Besides, we're expecting Dr. Dan to come for dinner tonight. I think I'm beginning to like him a lot. What do you think of him?"

He's a good human.

Liz laughs, "He probably thinks I'm just a crazy pet owner because I say you talk to me. But, we know how funny that really is, don't we Kip? You're more like a partner than a pet."

Partner? That's good, I like that.

Smiling, Liz lifts her hand and slaps the golden stone in the cliff face and shouts, "I declare this run good and done." As the two turn around to move off the slab, the scene around them changes radically and they are instantly surrounded by pounding surf. Almost immediately, a high roller sweeps over the flat stone slab and soaks them. Grabbing hold of Kip's collar to keep him from being swept away in the surge, Liz jams the fingers her other hand into a narrow crevasse in the cliff face.

Terrified by this wild unknown beach, Liz holds Kip close to her and presses them both against the cliff face. Looking south, she sees the point where her cabin should be is nothing but a bare outcropping of basalt that's being plummeted by the crashing waves. Turning to watch the waves rolling in from the west, Liz sees that the high red cliffs of her Redcliff's Beach north point are now massive sea-stacks standing against white-capped rollers crashing against their base.

Then these same waves rush towards the granite slab where she is holding onto Kip and Liz turns her back to the spray. Then, looking over her left shoulder, Liz sees the touchstone has moved up into the center of a wide arched opening with a staircase rising upwards. Instantly, Kip pulls from her hold and runs into the opening, bounding up the stairs.

"Kip wait for me." Liz shouts as she runs after him. To her surprise, the stairwell is lit by some unseen light source and, because of this, she can see each step is carved into the rock of the cliffs. Calling Kip as she runs, she hears his answering barks coming from somewhere above. Relieved that he is responding to her shouts, she calls him until she sees him sitting on the last step in the stairwell. This time he barks three times in a row and smile a wrinkle-nosed grin as she drop down beside him.

Wrapping her arms around his neck, Liz holds him for a long hug, then says, "Don't you ever run from me again. I thought I'd lost you forever. You must stay with me whenever something strange like this happens. Do you know where we are?"

It's a good place. You are safe here with me.

When she hears his words this time, Liz does not comment but slowly looks around where they are sitting. From there, she sees they are at the entrance into a wide hallway which is brightly lit by the same flashes of light that lit the stairwell. What is so beautifully done that it seems normal is the entire hallway, walls and floors, are covered with the purest white marble she has ever seen. Seeing the exquisite workmanship, she asks, "This looks as if it's been finished just the other day. Is it very old?"

I know this cave, dear one. It's a good place.

This time Kip's answer seems strange and she stares into his eyes. In that moment, Kip gives her cheek a swipe with his tongue, then stands and barks once before he trots halfway down the hallway. When he stops, Kip barks three times and bounces with excitement. Hurrying to him, the dog nudges her to turn to the left and, in that instant, Liz sees a deep alcove in the side wall where there are three white marble statues of nude men standing over twelve feet high with various animals surrounding them. Each male statue holds a massive bundle on one shoulder filled with scrolls, tools, or weapons.

When Liz starts to question Kip, the dog barks three times and nudges her to turn to the other side of the hall where she sees another alcove which holds three marble statues of nude women in various stages of motherhood. These also stand twelve feet high with many babies and children around their feet. Each of these female statues holds a large basket on their heads which are filled with either fruits, flowers, or vegetables.

All these statues stare across the hallway, as if daring the opposite side to come across the hallway. Mesmerized by what she sees, Liz forgets where she is and stares at the magnificent forms for several minutes. It is Kip's three sharp barks that bring her back to the present and she hurries to where he stands at the end of the hallway and says, "Thank you for showing me those beautiful statues, Kip. They're so exquisite. I'm amazes to find them in here."

You'll meet them again. Now, follow me. You have much to see.

"Kip, do you know this cave?"

I have been here many lifetimes.

Startled by the dog's revelation, Liz asks, "Kip? Is this why you came to me? Are you to show me what I am to know? If so, I'm counting on you to know the way back home. Where are we going?"

As I said, follow me.

At that, the dog turns and trots ahead of her, Liz asks, "Kip? Did you see how those statues seemed to move without actually moving?"

Without answering her, Kip stops and looks up at the ceiling. Following his gaze, Liz sees the bright flashes of light that have been dancing across the ceiling and down the stairwell. Liz shouts, "That's it. The moving lights make the statues seem to move. But, how does the light get in here? How can it be this bright so deep inside the cliffs?"

As if his answer, Kip barks once and disappears around the curve at the end of the hall. Running after him, Liz finds the dog sitting in front of a wide opening where brilliant flashes of light emerge and cover the walls and ceiling. Along the top of the walls, Liz sees carved openings and exclaims, "That's how the stairwell was lit. The light goes out through those openings to the stairwell and the hallway we were in. But, that doesn't tell me where the light comes from."

This time Kip nudges her into the brilliant light and Liz squints to see what he wants to show her. Through the opening where the light is the most brilliant, Liz sees a massive room with masses of crystals of various shapes and sizes covering the walls and ceiling. As she tries to enter the room, she is stopped by a huge crystal grouping which blocks the entrance.

When the light dims suddenly, Kip barks and looks up. Doing the same, Liz sees a large opening in the ceiling of the huge room beyond. "Kip, it's that opening that lets sunlight into the cave. Then it hits the facets on all those crystal groupings and bounces from facet to facet until it comes through this large opening. That's why the light flashes and why this space is so well lit. Without that opening, it would be totally dark in here."

As she looks at the endless crystal formations within the massive space, something causes a break in the sunlight coming through the skylight and, that one blink of shadow, creates a flash of light that rebounds throughout the crystal room in nanoseconds. Each flash rebounding from facet to facet, over and over again and again.

"My God, Kip. This is beautiful. It's easy to see why the stairs and hallway were so well lit and why the statues seemed to move. Even the millions of teeny crystals formed around this wide opening catch the light and seem to dance. Do you know if there's a way to get into that large space beyond these large crystals? It's as if the cave only wants us to see the crystals and not touch what's inside."

Suddenly Liz exclaims, "Kip, look at the edge around this wide opening. That crystal room is actually a giant geode. See how these tiny crystals were formed naturally around the opening. Except for its massive size, this opening looks exactly like the one on that geode Peter brought back from Peru three years ago. It almost covers my coffee table and I thought it was huge. Heck. Kip, this geode is massive."

Touching the sharp pointed tips of the tiny crystals massed over the large round opening, Liz says, "There must be billions of crystals around this opening. Look how these tiny crystals mesh together, building on or wrapping around each other, yet each seems to be in their own perfect place. Damn, I wish we could get inside and look at those crystals back there. I'd love to see the whole cave up close."

Completely fascinated, Liz touches the giant crystal formation that blocks her entry into the massive room and touches its largest facet. At that moment, the sun shines through the large opening in the ceiling and she is nearly blinded by the intensity of light rebounding off the thousands upon thousands of crystal formations. Closing her eyes, Liz cries out, "Kip, don't look at the light. Look down at the floor. Come here. Let me cover your face with my scarf."

Taking the cotton scarf from around her neck, she reaches to cover the dog's face. However, Kip pulls away from her hands and says,

I do not need this, dear one. You use it.

Holding the scarf out to her, Kip says,

My eyes are used to the brightest of light.

Taking it from him, Liz ties it over her own eyes and tells him, "You're so right my friend, this is much better. Now I can see what's ahead of me. How many times have you been here?"

As I said, many lifetimes.

Then the dog trots away and goes to the last facet on the huge crystal blocking the entrance into the geode. When Liz follow him, he suddenly disappears. Unable to see where he went, she shouts, "Kip, where did you go? Kip?"

Instantly, Kip's head appears between the last facet of the huge crystal and the basalt wall of the cliffs. Barking once, he tells her,

Bend low and you'll see the pathway to follow.

When Liz does this, she sees a glowing tiles that flash with many colors. Stunned by the beauty of the stone tiles, Liz kneels to touch them and sees they are made of fire opals. Smoothing her hands across the rare gems, she asks, "Kip? Do you realize these wonderful tiles are made from fire opals?"

Yes, dear one. They are part of the perfection of this crystal room. Now get up and follow me.

After telling her this, Kip nudges her down the glowing path. Following the animal, Liz sees she is in a massive cave covered with thousands and thousands of crystal formations of various sizes and shapes. For several minutes, she is so dumbfounded by what she sees, she stands and turns slowly around and around. Finally, Kip comes back and repeatedly nudges her along the path of fire-opal tiles to where it opens into a wide circular floor in the center of the crystal room.

Tears slipping down her cheeks, Liz whispers, "Oh Kip. This is so amazingly. It's the most beautiful place I've ever seen."

Staring from the crystals hanging overhead to the fire-opals tiles under her feet, Liz continues until she stops next to Kip who is standing in the center of a wide circular fire-opal tiled floor. Staring around the massive space, she sees the fire-opal tiles move with deep reds, brilliant yellows and royal blues. Each color is flecked with flashes of gold and white, never being still. Bemused, Liz begins to turn slowly in one spot so she can see the colors move within the tiles.

It is then that she see the sunlight is coming through the opening to the cave's ceiling at an angle due to the early hour and only hits the crystals on the far side the room. Taking the scarf from off her eyes, Liz exclaims, "Kip, this room is breath taking, absolutely beautiful. Thank you for bringing me here. I'm truly awed. It's the most exquisite place I've ever seen. This fire-opal tiled floor is especially amazing. Each of these tiles glows as if on fire. Where in the world would anyone find so many fire opals? I thought they were only found in Australia. This room must have been built by very special people, for very special people. Kip, do you know who they were? Were you here when they did all this?"

Though the dog looks directly at her as she asks her questions, he does not answer. Instead, he trots a ways from her and begins to turn slowly as if chasing his tail. After several turns, he stops, looks at Liz and says,

Come, do this with me and you will know what you ask.

Without another question, Liz goes to stand beside him and when he begins to turn again, so does she.

At that time, she sees subtle signs of wear on the fire-opal tiles around the room and she says, "Kip, look over there. Do you see the wear on those tiles? There had to be many walking over those tiles, for many years, for them to show that sort of wear on them. Do you know how long ago people first came here? Do you understand what I'm asking?"

Yes. They came thousands of years ago through the wormhole and they come often. Just as we came today.

The dog's words stop Liz and she stares at Kip even though he continues to turn upon the flashing tiles. Shaking her head, Liz begins to turn again. It is then that clouds covering the sun causes the light in the crystal room dims and she can see across the whole room. There, at the edge of the fire-opal tiled floor, is a bench cut from the granite of the cliffs. Following it with her eyes, she sees it goes all along the wall to end at a set of carved steps going up to the opening in the cave's ceiling.

"Kip, there's a stone bench that follows the far wall, then changes into a set of stairs going up to the opening in the ceiling. That opening looks as if it's also a natural part of the giant geode. That must be how the people found this wonderful cave. They must have looked in from above and decided this crystal room was magic and used the room to perform miracles during their ceremonies."

Suddenly, Liz stops turning and sits down on the tiles in the center of the room and moans, "Whoa, Kip. I'm too dizzy. Whew. I've got to sit and get my equilibrium back. Please, Kip, stop turning. You're making me ill."

When he stops turning, Kip comes to sit beside her and says,

When you turn, close your eyes and the crystals will talk to you and you won't become ill.

"Why we were turning anyway? Is there something magical you want me to experience? Kip?"

Though the dog doesn't answer, Liz continues speaking, more to herself than to the dog. "Think of the distance these people must have traveled to bring everything to the crystal room. It boggles my mind."

They brought everything with them through the wormhole at the base of the thrones.

Stunned by his words, Liz stares at Kip and waits for him to tell her more. Instead, he walks to the far side of the room and looks up. When Liz follows him and does the same, she sees what she hadn't noticed before. In between a pair of magnificent crystal formations there are two exquisitely carved thrones embedded with jewels of many types. Each of the surrounding crystals are aquamarines.

Reaching up, Liz touches the closest formation and says, "How amazing these are. It doesn't take much imagination to realize the people who developed this crystal room had a hierarchy. These thrones alone show that whoever sat in them were thought to be special people, possibly even as gods."

Completely awestruck, Liz walks from one side of the formation to the other, staring at each in wonder. Suddenly, she exclaims, "Kip, look here. There are stairs going up this side of the thrones. The workmanship is the same excellent work done on the stairwell coming into the cave, not one facet has been broken. Exceptional sculptors or jewelers did this work. Oh, Kip, how I would love to meet the people who built this and hear their stories. Will I meet them someday? Will that ever happen?"

Probably in one of your next lifetimes.

This time, Liz stares at the dog but does not to question his remark. Her instincts tell her that Kip knows much more than he'll ever tell her and she realizes it's more than she wants to know. In order to control of her unease, Liz turns away from the thrones and points at the opening in the ceiling. "Kip, the sun's nearly overhead, I think it's time for us to go back home. Do you know how to get back there?"

Barking once, Kip trots across the fire-opal tiles and goes up the stairs carved along the sidewall. Then he stands in the opening at the top and stares down at her. Following him to where he waits, Liz asks, "Why didn't you go through the opening? Don't you want to be first out of the cave?"

Kip doesn't answer her, but gently nudges her ahead of him until Liz steps through the opening and shouts, "Kip. We're in the State Park on the cliffs above our own Redcliff's Beach."

When she goes to the cliff edge and looks down at the beach, Kip trots down the road and waits. Going to where he has stopped, Liz sees a sign on the pole fence around the State Park's main attraction and laughs, "Kip, we've come out that old lava tube I used to climb into when I was a kid. I certainly never saw crystals down there, not one. Let's go down to the beach and run home. See the green of our old copper roof?"

The excited dog barks three times and spins in circles, then runs ahead of her through the park's entry gate and down to the beach. She catches up with him at the edge of the waves and Kip greets her with his three barks and a wrinkled nose grin. Laughing, Liz kneels to hug him and says, "I think you're more relieved to be back than I am, Kip. Thank you for showing me that wonderful crystal room. It was amazing."

Giving her left ear several licks, the large dog snuggles into her arms and heaves a big sigh. Liz whispers, "I agree, Kip, it was a great adventure, but it's good to be back home, safe and sound. Besides, I'm hungry and I'll bet you are too."

Let's run home.

Late that afternoon, Liz takes a break from writing about being a Parallel Life of Elizabeth Ann. After she closes her computer, she gets a glass of iced tea and goes out to the deck with Kip following behind. As she pulls her favorite chaise lounge into the shade and starts to sit down, the big dog whines until she pulls the other chaise beside her. Then Kip jumps onto the chaise, heaves a big sigh and closes his eyes.

Enjoying the sight of such a wonderful animal feeling so safe and cared for, Liz closes her own eyes and sighs as a soft breeze caresses her cheeks. Nearly asleep, she is startled away by loud voices coming from somewhere on the beach. Sitting up, she looks out at the beach to see what the excitement is about and sees nothing unusual. Still hearing the shouts, she looks up to the north and sees a crowd has gathered below the north cliffs. Though she can see several people pointing at the cliff face, the loudest voice is, again, coming from the house next door to hers.

Getting up she goes to the end of the deck and sees the same man on the deck of the house directly to the north of hers. This time the man waves his arms wildly and yells into his hand. Liz decides he is yelling into a cellphone and upset about something on the cliffs. Reaching inside the slider, she slips her binoculars off their hook and scans the cliff face.

There, along one of the highest ledges on the cliff face, is the same woman she'd seen fighting off attacking birds last week. However, this time the woman dangles precariously off the ledge. One hundred and fifty feet below her lays the granite slab Liz runs to every morning. This time the woman is struggling to pull her backside back onto the ledge. Swinging her right leg upwards, she is trying to catch the edge of the ledge with her foot. Finally, she does and manages to slowly pull herself onto the ledge. When she is laid full length along the ledge, she does nothing but breathe for several minutes.

All the while the woman lies still, the crowd gathered on the beach shout and cheer wildly. After she's laid still for several minutes, the crowd grows restless and begins to shout directions or make catcalls. Ignoring them all, the woman takes her time getting onto her hands and knees. Then, very slowly, she begins to back along the ledge until she is stopped by a ragged outcropping. Then, just as slowly, the woman turns towards the cliff face and stands. Inching up the outcropping, she pulls herself upwards, one careful step at a time.

When the woman finally reaches the top edge of the cliff face, the crowd goes wild. Ignoring the commotion below, the woman methodically rolls herself away from the edge, then crawls a dozen feet more before standing up beside a picnic table. At first she brushes the dirt off her knees, then walks back to the edge of the cliff top and waves to the crowd below, shouting something that causes them to cheer wildly.

Laughing while relief, Liz says, "She made it, Kip. That bird woman got herself out of another bad situation. Her husband's not on their deck anymore. He must have gone up to the State Park. Yup. There he is beside her and he's hugging her. Now it looks as if they're both crying. That's a good thing to do as I know I would if that were me."

Those two are Dan's friends.

"You're right. I should call him and give him a heads-up and ask him to invite them for dinner tonight. That way we'll get to meet them and hear her story. What do you think about that?"

Good plan of attack.

"What? Do you think it's too obvious that we'd like to see him again?"

We?

Looking at Kip, Liz blushes a bit then hangs up the field glasses and hurries to the phone to dial Dr. Parker's number. When he gets on the line, she tells him what happened and asks if he and his friends would come to dinner that evening. He accepts with a deep chuckle and again she blushes. Then, Liz pointedly adds to remember to bring his friends so she can meet them.

Thanking her for the invitation, Dr. Parker says he'd love to come for dinner and will most certainly ask his friends to come with him. After hanging up, Liz hurries to the kitchen to see if there is enough food to fix a decent meal for four.

FIVE

June 5th—Beth

BETH reaches the north cliffs just as the sun breaks over the Coastal Mountain Range and the first rays are so brilliant she immediately turns towards the large translucent agate in the cliff face. Leaning her forehead onto the glowing stone, she listens to whatever messages the stone has for her that morning and when it's finished, she slaps the golden stone and shouts, "I declare this run good and done."

It's then that scraping sounds off to her left catch her attention. Looking out past the cliff point, she sees Lucy Wong digging into the exposed tidal flats near the edge of the outgoing tide. The bright pinks and golds of the sunrise reflect off Lucy's white shirt and shorts making them seem effervescent. Beth shouts a greeting but her words are drowned out by the din of seabirds landing around Lucy to peck through discarded shovelfuls tossed back to the tide flats. Wading through the tide flats, Beth watches the birds landing and flapping around her friend and laughs, "Holy cow, it's the mad scientist in all her glory."

When she is a few feet behind Dr. Wong, Beth shouts again and this time the woman turns towards her holding out a shovelful and shouts, "Have you ever seen such a load of sea life on one shovel?"

Nodding, Beth shouts back, "That's the very reason Maxine wanted this area turned into a Preserve. Amazing isn't it?"

Tossing the shovelful onto a screen, Lucy shakes off the sand and lifts up the screen to show Beth the various sized clams, shrimp, and tiny crabs scattered over it. Picking through the booty, she drops the chosen specimens into a thick waterproof sack tied to her belt, then tosses the discards into the hole they'd been dug from, now filled with seawater.

Giving a thumbs up sign, Beth points at the bulging sack of sea life and asks Lucy, "When are you going to take that load up? That sack looks pretty heavy."

"Right now. This low tide is amazing. Ever see such a load of clams? I'll dissect several of each type and have the rest for dinner." Lucy shouts, pointing at the sack hanging down to her toes, "It's a bother to have to tie this on me, but if I use a bucket, the damn birds get in it and dump it over."

"Looks as if it's a good showing for your first dig. Is it?"

Lucy laughs, "More than good, Beth. This is the richest beach I've seen south of Alaska. I'm going up to the trailer right now and make a formal count of what I've got. Then I'll come back and collect till high tide at noon. This month the tides are to be the highest and lowest of the century."

"That's right! I forgot about that."

"High tide isn't until noon. So it gives me lots of time to sample several areas on the beach. Some of the clams I'll use to replant the areas Tom Ames scraped off to build the sand dunes. The head of my department is coming next month to see how I'm situated. I want to show him the quality of the beach to the north as well. It's an amazing little cove. I'll bet smugglers used it at one time."

"Don't be too surprised it they still do," Beth nods, "It'd be great if that beach could be part of Maxine's preserve. That's where I'm going now. Keep your eyes on the time and don't get caught too far out when the tide turns. See you later."

Leaving Lucy at the edge of the outgoing tide, Beth walks back to the end of the point and stops at the edge of a deep pool that reaches under the cliff point. As she wades along its edge, the teal green seawater ripples with each of her steps. Suddenly a small octopus slides out from under a large rock and flees backwards into the shadows under the cliff point. Inspired by the sight, Beth wade in up to her knees, takes a large breath then slips underwater to peer into the lush sea garden of anemones and starfish under the cliff. Swimming down, she sees the octopus inside an old green bottle has changed skin color to match that of the shadowed undercut. Surfacing, she scares schools of tiny fish which flash away to the deepest shadows only to be caught by the sea life living down there.

As she works her way around the immense tide pool, Beth angles towards the wide sandbar flowing out from the sloping shoreline. Letting the sun and breeze dry her clothes, she notices when the wind dies completely and sees a perfect reflection of the cliff tops are laid on the surface, showing the bluest of skies in the background. The beautiful scene puts her in such a tranquil mood, that when a hard gust of wind erases the reflection, she is startled and turns to look back past the cliff point.

It's then that she realizes there is a silence that is not normal. It's too total and Beth it struck by a strong urgency to hurry towards shore. Walking briskly across the sandbar connected to the shoreline, she is almost running when the ground gives a strange shift of movement and the sloping sandbar suddenly drops below a high bank of rocks and boulders. Looking at the cliff point, she sees high rolling waves are crashing against several tall sea stacks where the cliff point used to be.

"Sea stacks, what the hell...? This beach doesn't have sea stacks. There's only one cliff point at each end of Redcliff's beach. In my dimension... damn, the dimension must have changed. This isn't my beach. Not anymore. And the tide's coming in fast."

Scrambling across tide flats now covered with rocks and boulders, Beth tries to reach the giant boulders along the high cut of the shoreline. However within those few seconds, the beach sinks and the first high rolling wave hits, knocking her off her feet. Struggling against the push of the fast water, Beth's legs and knees scrape against barnacle covered boulders and float logs as she tries to push towards shore. Soon she is caught in the powerful backflow of the waves and is pulled away from shore.

Swimming with the surge, Beth tries her best to stay close to shore, but each time she is pushed and pulled past boulders covered with barnacles and gobs of muscles which cut and scrape her arms and legs. When she is finally able to grab onto a smooth boulder sticking out of the water, she holds herself there and is able to rest a few minutes. However, a massive wave sweeps around the sea stacks, crashes over her and sucks her under water for nearly a minute. Kicking her way back to the surface, she is pulled back across sharp edged mussels clinging to unseen boulders.

Crying out as the sea life slashes her hands and legs, Beth kicks away and tries to swim with the force of the wave. As soon as she is swept towards shore and nearly reaches safety, the wave catches her in the retreating back flow pulling her past where she'd been. Floundering in the fast flowing water, Beth feels tentacles wrap her legs and realizes she is caught in a bed of whipping kelp. Now exhausted, she lays back upon the swaying whips of the seaweed and lets the kelp forest hold her against the push/pull of each wave.

It takes another high rolling wave to pull her free from the kelp forest's hold and Beth lets herself be pulled towards shore. Too exhausted to struggle, she turns onto her back and lets the force of the ocean pull her to and fro on each swell. Slowly, the waves bring her closer to the high cut of shoreline where a row of sun-bleached drift logs rest beside several large boulders.

This when a huge half-submerged float log, riding within a rushing wave, broadsides Beth and knocks her unconscious. As the giant log pushes against her, a snag grabs hold of Beth's tee-shirt and secures her firmly to its surface. When the old floater nears shore, it slowly rolls within the wave, turning upside down, and pulls Beth under the water for the time it takes the wave to leave the log on shore. The wave reaches its peak flow above the shoreline and the log rolls once more, bringing Beth's limp body to the surface with her T-shirt held tight by the snag. In the next few seconds, the wave settles the old floater between immense boulders on the steep shoreline and the impact of the landing wakens Beth.

Finding herself dangling over a pile of sun bleached logs, Beth realizes she is on dry solid ground and she struggles to sit up and feels something holding onto her. Jerking this way and that, she finally frees her tee-shirt and slides off the side of the log with a hard bounce on the logs below. Springing to her feet, Beth, powered by a rush of adrenaline, ignores her injuries and scrambles through the boulders to a zig-zagging path along a rocky slope.

Following this path up to where an old stump stands rooted at the edge of a smooth section of granite, Beth stops and leans against the stumps smooth silver surface. Feeling warmth from the sun-heated wood, she slowly sits down on the smooth granite and tares at the waves crashing over the boulders where the float log was laid. Seeing how close she came to death, Beth shivers and hunkers into the folds of the stump's thick twisted roots.

It's then that she sees the slashes across her legs, arms and hands and gently tries to brush sand from the tender wounds. Her efforts reopen the wounds and cause them to bleed. Pulling off the torn tee-shirt, she dabs at the bloody gashes until the blood flow stops. Feeling the warmth of the sun upon her bare skin, Beth strips off the rest of her clothing and spreads it over the rocks around her. The bloody tee-shirt is flipped over the nearest twisted root. Naked, but much warmer, Beth lays back against the sun-heated granite surface of the cliff and the warmth soothes her bruised body. Within minutes, she is sound asleep.

The sun is high in the sky when a pair of terns scream down at her from the top of the old stump and waken Beth. At first she is confused as to where she is and why she is totally naked. Then, seeing her clothes spread out around her, she remembers and finds each piece warm and dry as she dresses.

Checking the wounds on her legs and arms, she decides not to touch the dried slashes and looks up at the sky. "I'd guess, by the angle of the sun, it must be nearly noon. By the looks of the burn on my arms, I must have slept over an hour. I'd better find my way back home and get some aloe on them."

Standing, she startles the terns off their next at the top of the stump and as she watches the pair flap away, she sees the old giant log, which brought her to shore, is bobbing at the edge of the highest tide she's ever seen. Frowning at where the log is floating, Beth realizes if it had not rolled her back the surface before it settled between those boulders, she would have been crushed or drowned.

"But I wasn't." Beth tells herself and gives the old thing a salute and says, "Thanks for the ride old friend. You did all the right things. Many thanks for saving my life."

Looking up the switchback path, she sees it rises to the top of the cliffs. "But, will it take me back to my dimension? Will Lucy be there? Did she notice I was gone? Would she have sent for help?"

Then snorting a laugh, Beth answers herself, "Lot of good that would do, Beth, not even Liz and Eliza would know where to look for me. I'll have to find my own way home and going over the cliff top is the only option I have. Maybe I'll luck out and find my own Redcliff's Beach on the other side."

As she works her way up the trail, Beth begins to see a stone structure is stretching along the cliff tops. At the last turn in the trail, she sees it is a high wall of stacked stones. The closer she gets the higher the structure grows until she is standing at one end of the wall. The she can see how it was built to curve to the south at both ends and has a long bench built into the curve of the wall.

"Probably to protect it from the north winds. How lovely." she murmurs sitting down on the long stone bench and leaning back against the stone wall's inner curve. In front of this bench sits a long curving table made from driftwood and stones which also follows the curve of the bench. Running her fingers across the smooth wood surfaces, Beth is awed by the quality of each structure.

At the far end of the wall sits a large stone fireplace with a high chimney and an iron grate over the firebox. A slight spiral of smoke and the heat from the grate tells her a fire was lit that morning. To the east, Beth sees a thickly forested hillside. At the bottom of the hillside, a wide trail runs along the shoreline going north and south. At the bottom of the cliffs, the trail zips straight up the hill to the cliff tops.

That's when she notices that halfway up, the trail makes a sharp turn and goes up through the forest. Shading her eyes against the sunlight, she sees the trail ends at a white house amongst tall trees. Letting her eyes follow the path to the south, she sees it ends at a point where her own home would be. Instead, there is only a massive basalt flow which breaks off at a high shoreline to form three low sea stacks of basalt march away from shore. Studying these, Beth sees that the largest and furthest stack from shore has a flat surface.

"That flat area could be the cement floor Dad poured for his cabin. If so, another Elizabeth Ann lives in that house on the hill. Yes, there has to be. Why else would I be brought into this dimension? Maybe she's the person Eliza saw run into a cave that opened in the cliff face. No, it couldn't be. Eliza said that cave exited onto a beach of golden sand. The beach back where I washed up on today is nothing but rocks. My poor shins and hands are testimony to that."

Returning to the sun heated bench, Beth leans back against the stone wall and thinks over the possibilities of how to find her way home and who would else would live in this dimension. Daydreaming, she does not see movement to her right and is startled to her feet when a loud voice demands, "Who the hell are you and why are sitting on my bench staring down at my beach?"

As soon as she stands, Beth is knocked back to the bench by a large golden dog that leaps beside her and pushes her against the stone wall. Growling deep in its throat, the large animal stares at her with its golden eyes. Holding the dog back with both hands, Beth turns towards the voice and sees a woman stepping through the tall sea grasses. Gasping with delight, she also sees that the woman looks exactly as an Elizabeth Ann Anderson should, in every way.

Pleased to have guessed right about who would live in this dimension, Beth exclaims, "You're Elizabeth Ann Anderson, aren't you?

I'm sure you are. I am, too. Look at me, do you see that you and I look exactly alike? I'd recognize you anywhere."

At the sound of her voice, the large dog stops growling and lies down on the bench, eyeing Beth with a puzzled tilt of its head. Instead of answering Beth's question, the woman repeats her own question, "I said, who the hell are you and what are you doing sitting on my bench?"

As Beth begins to answer, the woman cries out, "Oh my God, you are me! How can you be so like me? Who are you? How did you get here? Where did you come from?"

Beth takes a deep breath and says, "I'm Elizabeth Ann Anderson. I'm known as Beth to my friends and family. I have a sister named Dana Marie who calls herself Dee. She is two years older than I am. I live at Redcliff's Beach in the cabin my father, James Anderson, built for his wife Jill and his daughters when I was just a baby.

"Last year, two Parallel Lives came to me and we've discovered we're from the same original child named Elizabeth Ann Anderson. The other two women are named Liz Day and Eliza Staples. We each live within different dimensions, just as you live in this dimension. This morning, I was swept into this dimension by an incoming tide and managed to swim to safety on the north shore. I knew the dimension had changed as the beach over there is nothing but rocks and boulders. In my dimension, the beach is narrow and nearly all sand.

"Even though I knew the tides were to be extreme, I got too interested in a wonderful tide pool and got caught by the incoming tide. I almost drowned. An old drift log smashed against me and knocked me out. When I woke up I found myself on shore still on top of the log. Waves crashed over boulders near me and I was terrified. I climbed the steep slope to an old tree stump, stripped off my wet clothes and was so exhausted I fell asleep. When I woke, I came up here to see if I could find a way back home to my own dimension.

"I love what you've done here. You are the one who built everything, aren't you? It's all really wonderful. Did you build them yourself?"

When Beth gestures towards the structures, the dog wags its tale and sniffs at her fingers. "Is there a touchstone in the cliff face below us? If so I'm sure I can find my way back home. This is the first time I've gone into another dimension and it scares me."

At this time, Beth stops talking and waits. However, after several minutes of being stared at without a word spoken to her, Beth points south and asks, "Does that flat section on the largest basalt piece have the cement floor Dad poured for his cabin? If so, is the large golden stone he imbedded in the west end still there? It's that stone where each of our homes connect at the adjoined dining tables over the stone. It seems our dimension have meshed together at that point. We three meet there daily over that golden stone. Maybe you could try to sit there and come through to us. Would you like to try?"

Without answering, the woman rushes to Beth and sits next to her. Then after comparing each freckle or mole on their arms, she places her head in her hands and sobs loudly. Startled by her reaction, Beth lays an arm around the woman's shaking shoulders and says, "Don't be sad. You'll like us. We're just like you are in many ways."

As she speaks, the large blonde dog puts its head on Beth's knee and, with one arm around the woman, Beth automatically pats the dog's head with the other hand as she continues to talk softly to the woman "There, there, don't be frightened. I'm a real person. You aren't crazy. I felt the same way when I first met Liz and Eliza. It was so strange to meet other women who looked exactly the same as I do and not know them."

Slowly, the woman turns and looks up at Beth for a long while. Finally, she sits up and says, "You are here, aren't you? You're not a spook. I can feel your arm around me and your hand on my shoulder. You must be real. Tell me again about the other women named Elizabeth Ann Anderson."

Beth repeats what she said before, then she tells about herself and when she meets the others at the adjoined tables. Finally, she stops and asks, "What is your name? Would you tell me about yourself?"

The woman says, "I'm Ann Anderson. I dropped Elizabeth years ago when I became a TV announcer/writer. Ann Anderson made a better sign off name. My family, my mother, my father and sister Dana were killed when a drunk driver smashed into our car. I was fourteen. I was asleep in the back seat and was knocked out. I didn't wake up until the rescue people found me. Even then I didn't know anything had happened until they told me. It was horrible. I was so alone and so frightened.

"I went to live in Salem with my Aunt Margret. We were very close until she passed away ten years ago. When, I graduated from college I took a job at a Portland TV station and worked my way up to the nightly news and specials. I have a small condo in Portland for late nights or bad weather. However, that house on the hill is my real home.

"Redcliff's Beach is where we spent most of our lives and the last hours together. I lived in Dad's cabin for years until a massive tsunami ripped down the coastline. They said it was caused by a nine point five plus quake in British Columbia. It killed thousands of people up and down the coast. Fortunately for me, it hit when I was at work in Portland.

"In one short hour, everything that was Redcliff's Beach, houses, motels, and businesses, were gone. All the high sand dunes that covered the full six miles of beach were swept away. At that time, I started this wall as a way to work out my pain of losing Dad's cabin. It seemed everything was gone. I contacted the State and they let me buy the strip of frontage along the miles of beach. Above me is mostly National Forest with an odd section or two along my land due to old homesteads."

As Ann talks, Beth feels the woman's grip tighten around her, "You must stay here with me, Beth. If you go, I will never see you again. Please, understand. I can't take the chance of losing you."

Not saying a word, Beth smiles sweetly and leans into the woman's arms trying to think of a plan. However, when she feels Ann's arm drop from around her shoulders, Beth pushes her away and dashes to the trail she'd seen go down the slope to the beach. Never looking back, Beth runs as fast as she can to the rocky beach and picks her way through the rocks with a determination she didn't know she had. When she reaches the granite slab at the base of the cliffs, she sees a soft glow under a growth of moss along the cliff face. Scrubbing at the stone with both hands, she cleans the stone until it shines brilliantly. Then she slaps it and screams, "I declare this run good and done."

A second later, she is standing on the granite slab at the bottom of the north red cliffs on her Redcliff's Beach. Trembling with relief, Beth slides down against the cliff face and stares at everything around her. She is where she should be. She is home. To the south, her cabin sits on its basalt point exactly where her Dad had built it. Turning to her left, she sees Lucy's trailer with its big diesel truck parked behind it at the end of the Shoreline Drive turnaround.

In that instant, she also sees Lucy Wong running across the narrow slice of sand, waving her arms and shouting at her. "Where did you go? Where did you go? I looked everywhere for you. I went around the point where you did, but you were nowhere to be seen. I even hiked to the top of the cliffs to see if I could find you from there. I shouted and whistled and screamed. Finally, I gave up and went back to collecting sea-life until the tide came at me. Damn it, Beth, you have no idea what a scare you gave me. Where did you go after you went around the point? It's not funny, Beth, I was so worried about you. Why are you laughing?"

Beth says, "Because, Lucy, I just realized you are so right. I do need to tell you what happened to me this morning and what has happened for a whole year now. Will you drive me home? I'll fix us lunch and tell you everything that has happened to me, today and before. I'll also explain who and what I am. Will you take me home, now?"

After the two women have eaten and are again settled at the dining table, Beth says, "Ask me any questions as they come to you, Lucy. I'll answer them as I go along so I can be sure that you understand. Also know that what I'm going to tell you is the whole truth as I know it. Please, remember that. I will not edit out anything that's happened to me. All I ask is that you keep an open mind and be assured that I'm not crazy. These adventures began the day that my darling, Maxine, died one year ago…"

For the rest of the afternoon, Lucy listens to Beth's story. When Lucy asks a question, Beth answers. Finally, Beth explains what happened to her that very morning and ends her tale with the moment Lucy saw her leaning against the cliff face.

"And that's all I have to say about me for now. Why don't we take a break? I'll make a pot of tea and cut more brownies, would you like that?"

"That'd be great." Lucy nods, "Besides, I can't think of anything else to ask. As for you telling the truth, who could ever make something like that up?"

"I've been so afraid to tell anyone about my real life as it's still so unexplainable to me. I've been afraid if you knew the truth, you'd hook up your trailer and tow it down to the south cliffs."

"I'm glad you decided to tell me. Now I won't worry if you disappear again, as you did today. When I first moved here, I wondered how you could be so content out here by yourself. Now I know you're not alone. Do you think I could ever meet Liz and Eliza?"

Beth laughs, "I won't say no, as I know anything is possible. Anything."

SIX

June 5th—Eliza

ELIZA throws the blankets aside feeling ready to face the day and swings her legs off the side of the bed and sits up. It's only then that she realizes she's in her sister's room and that's when the memory of losing Marie and the twins in the plane crash a week ago comes back with a smashing force that topples her back onto the pillows. Doubling into a fetal position as the heartache claims her body, she weeps loudly releasing the overwhelming pain of her loss. Words of love and loss tumble from her mouth as she beats the pillows, shouts and curses the Universe for allowing such a thing to happen to her loved ones.

Suddenly an angry voice penetrates her sorrow and stops her cold. *Stop making that racket, Eliza. Get yourself up and get going. Enough with the tears and the pitiful weeping. You don't mourn for me nor the twins, you mourn for your loss, not us. You make your own pain. The twins and I are with Mom and Dad and we all send our love to you. Know always that we watch over you. I've come back to tell you how wonderful it is on this side. You'll see for yourself soon, when you come over to us.*

Till then, Eliza, get up and get on with your life. Stop making my room a shrine. Go live in your own rooms and stay out of that pit of self-pity you're thrown yourself into. Empty my room of all my things. Take them to where others can use them. Get up now, Eliza. Go. Get on with your life.

Looking around the room, Eliza sees no one and says, "Marie? If that was really you, show yourself. Just once. I must see you before I'll believe you came into my mind just now."

Instantly, a shimmering orb appears a few feet in front of her. When Eliza reaches out to hold it with her hands, Marie's face appears within the glittering light. Holding the image in both her hands, Eliza feels a joyous ecstasy and knows it is Marie.

Dear Eliza, I've shown myself to you so that you know that I was the one who spoke. Now, I demand that you release me. The twins and I are needed by others. Jim is with us and both our parents, Jill and James Anderson. We are at home with them all. Know that you were and are loved, Eliza. Live your life to its fullest. Take great care to go where you are known. If you do that, you will live long and prosper. Know that you are loved.

At that, the shimmering orb vanishes from her hands. Instantly, Eliza forgets that Marie came to her and she immediately goes to her own rooms, showers, dresses, makes the bed then goes down to the kitchen and fixes her breakfast. After the dishes are in the dishwasher, she refills her coffee mug, takes it out to the railing of the beach deck and stands at the railing where she watches the activity along Redcliff's Beach.

As she sips the coffee, her eyes wander to the high north cliffs. "I wonder how things are with Liz and Beth. I haven't seen either of them for a couple weeks. Maybe I'll see them today."

Taking her mug back to the kitchen, she refills the coffeemaker with fresh beans and pushes the button. As the aroma of the fresh brew fills the room, a voice says, "Mm, that smells wonderful. Mind making a cup for me while you're at it."

Turning towards the voice, Eliza sees Beth sitting at the adjoined tables. Below her, Dandelion is snuggled on top of the golden stone. Delighted, Eliza says, "Sure thing, kiddo. Milk or sugar?"

"No, just black." Beth answers. "It's so good to see you. You're looking a lot better today than you did last week."

"Thanks, I am. Had a good cry this morning. I dreamt Marie told me to get on with my life and to stop making her room a shrine. Said to clear out her things and take them where others can use them. So that's what I'm going to do today. I might even take a run to the cliffs as I haven't done that for some time. Did you run today?"

Laughing, Beth says, "Hours ago. If you go, remember that the tides are extreme these next few weeks. This morning, I got so wrapped up looking at the tide pools, that I got caught by the incoming tide. The dimension changed and the waves got so wild and high I almost drowned. When I was finally washed ashore, I climbed to the top of those cliffs and met another Elizabeth Ann Anderson who lives there. She was so undone by me that she frightened me and I ran away.

"When I got back to Redcliff's Beach, Lucy demanded to know where I had gone. She drove me home and I told her everything about me, about us, our whole story, all of it. She's in the bathroom, right now. Maybe if you stay a bit longer, you'll get to meet her. Yes, here she is..."

As Eliza turns, Beth, Dandy and Lucy vanish. Shrugging, Eliza says, "So much for my meeting Lucy. Evidently it's not going to happen today."

Taking the fresh mug from under the coffeemaker, she adds milk and carries it out to the deck. As she walks to the railing, she sees a large white dog standing at the edge of the waves, looking her way. It's then that she remembers the white dog on the road the night the plane crash. Watching the animal, she notices people walk directly past the dog without noticing him. Intrigued, Eliza sets her mug on the railing and walks down the path through the dunes to where the dog waits at the edge of the waves.

As she gets closer, the animal begins to walk towards her. When the two are a few feet apart, the dog's golden eyes look into hers and seem to hold an intelligence that surprises her. "You're a beauty, aren't you? Are you a gift from Marie and the twins so I don't become too weird as I grow old and doddering? Or are you lost? You have the same golden eyes as Dandy and Kip do. Those two animals are 'familiars' to Beth and Liz. Have you come to be my 'familiar'?"

Kneeling in front of the animal, Eliza holds out her hand trying to encourage the animal to come to her. When it only stares at her, Eliza stands and says, "Well, I guess you're not mine so I'll say goodbye. I just buried my sister and her twins a few days ago and I have a lot to do. See you out on the beach, Whitey."

Going back to her deck, she picks up her coffee mug and empties it over the railing. As she walks up to the slider door, she notices the white dog doesn't show in the reflection of the beach yet when she turns around, she sees it sitting in the same spot she left it. Looking back at the reflection, she shivers and says to herself, "What the heck? He's out there but doesn't show here. I don't get it."

For the rest of the morning, Eliza works in Marie's room, filling box after box with her sister's things. After she's loaded the boxes into her car, she carries the dresses and coats down on their hangers and drapes them over the seats of the car. Once the BMW is as full as it can get, Eliza throws her purse onto the floor of the passenger side and starts the car.

Heading down Shoreline Drive, Eliza thinks about the white dog. When she gets to the four way stope in Ocean Shores, she turns right towards a thrift shop she where she's done a bit of shopping and decides to take Marie's things there. Parking in a space near the entrance of The Open Door Shoppe, she starts to get out of the car when she sees the white dog standing in front of the shop's doorway.

For some reason the fact that he's shown himself there, suddenly irritates Eliza and she shouts, "What the hell do you think you are doing there?" Her words startle a woman coming out from the shop and she shouts back, "Why the hell are you yelling at me? I don't even know you."

"I'm sorry, ma'am, I was yelling at that white dog."

"Lady, if you're seeing white dogs, you must be crazier than you sound. There's no white dog around here."

Shocked, Eliza asks, "You don't see the white dog standing next to your right leg?"

"No, I don't. There is no white dog to the right or to the left or straight ahead of me. Now let me past you or I'm going to scream for help."

Backing quickly to the front of her car, Eliza lets the frightened woman dash past her. Then Eliza hurries past the dog and pushes open the door of the shop, hissing at the dog, "You're not going to stop me today, buster. Nor any day. I'm getting on with my life."

When she pushes the door open, the animal vanishes and Eliza rushes inside the shop. Looking around the store as if not certain what she's should do, a young clerk at the cash-register asks, "Is there something I can help you with? You look as if you've seen a ghost."

Blinking back tears, Eliza says, "I've brought a load of my sister's things in my car. Marie died last week in a plane crash. Is there someone who can help me carry the boxes and clothes inside?"

"Of course, I'll get the manager." The clerk waves to a woman working at a desk at the back of the room. When the woman comes forward, she walks over to Eliza and coos, "I'm Mary Trimble, the shop manager, and how can I help you?"

Very quickly, the clerk explains why Eliza is there and the woman instantly turns towards the door, saying, "Come, Lisa, let's get her things inside so she doesn't have to wait any longer. Is your car open?" Seeing Eliza's nod, the two women prop the shop door open and help Eliza carry the boxes to the room at the back of the shop.

When they are finished, Mrs. Trimble makes a list of all the items and gives it to Eliza. "This receipt shows the number of things you've donated and the value I estimate they will sell for. Keep it for your taxes. It's what I'm sure we'll get for the items as they're so lovely. I thank you so much for bringing them to this shop. Their sales will help many needy women and children. I'm so grateful."

Eliza smiles at the woman, "Marie told me to give them where they would help others. I'm so glad you think they will. There is at least one more car load of things which I'll bring to you later. Not today, though. I didn't realize how hard it would be to give her things away. It's as if she just died all over again. I'll bring the rest of her things soon. Maybe next week."

The manager, Mary Trimble, wraps her arm around Eliza's shoulders and holds on to her for several seconds. When Eliza eases away and walks towards the shop's door. Mary Trimble follows her, saying, "My dear, take the time you need to heal before your next trip here. I know this will sound trite, but it's true, 'time heals all wounds'. You'll see for yourself what a difference each day makes. Take the days as they come, be kind to yourself and don't make any major decisions. It won't be easy for the next year. Each day will heal you a little more. Trust me, I speak from my own experience. If you want, come see me just to talk, I'm a good listener."

So moved by the woman's words, Eliza gives Mary Trimble a hug then dashes out to her car. As she backs out from the parking place, she sees the woman watching from the door of the shop. When the woman waves at her, Eliza smiles and realizes she may have found a new friend.

As she drives up Shoreline Drive, Eliza begins to think about the white dog and wonders aloud, "Will it be waiting for me at home? Did Marie send him to me? Are Jack and Peg's deaths the reason my sister and her girls died? They were so precious to me. Were they the payment for my sins? Who decides what will be? Why not take my life instead? Or is that too easy an out? Did I need to feel the horror of losing them? Was that it?"

Turning down her driveway, she pushes the remote to open the garage door and coasts into the garage. As soon as she has parked, the large white dog appears next to the door into her home. Sitting behind the steering wheel, she stares at the animal until the garage door closes. When the animal doesn't vanish or move away, Eliza slowly gets out of the car and goes up to the waiting dog. "Excuse me, Whitey," she tells the animal as she passes to go through the door into her home and carefully closes it behind her.

Walking through the house, Eliza leans on the dining table as she scans the beach and sees nothing of the white dog. Relieved, she turns towards the kitchen and instantly sees the large dog sleeping on the rug in front of the fireplace. At that moment, something clicks in Eliza and she goes over to the sleeping animal and demands, "Why are you following me? Are you trying to scare me? Well, doggy, I'll not be intimidated. I lived with that asshole Jack Staples for over thirty years and put up with enough shit from him for a dozen lifetimes. My killing him should make me a hero in the Universe. You and all the other entities should have applauded, not sentence the most precious people I knew to lose their lives. Why not kill me and send me to hell? Why kill my beautiful sister and her twins?"

When the dog only stares at her with its unblinking golden eyes, Eliza suddenly realizes something. "You're not here to judge me, are you? I don't feel a thing from you. You're waiting for me to do something. I'm right, aren't I? I have no reason to fear you, do I? Nothing at all."

When the dog shows no hint of responding to her, Eliza demands, "Look, if you're going to hang around me, the least you could do is speak to me as Kip does to Liz. Why follow me around and not say anything to me?"

Turning away from the dog, Eliza sees the sunset has turned a bright pink and she sighs, "Darling Marie, are you with me today? Let's go up to the W's lanai. I'll fix us tall gin and tonics and we'll watch the sunset together. Then, we'll talk and talk just you and me, as we used to do."

SEVEN

June 10ᵗʰ—Liz

LIZ fills Kip's food dish with kibble and says to him, "Having you run beside me each morning is such fun. Is it for you?"

Yes, I enjoy it.

While the dog eats its food, Liz makes a sandwich for herself and pours a cup of coffee. Taking both to the dining table, she hopes Beth and Eliza will come through to the adjoined tables while she's having her lunch. Staring out the window at the incoming waves of the high tide, she sees they are flattening for the next tidal change. Feeling Kip lay his head on her feet, she smiles and watches him curl his body round the golden stone in the floor. When he settles against her, they both heave sighs of contentment and Liz says, "My, gosh, Kip, we sound like a couple of old geezers. Don't we?"

She's here.

Before Liz can ask who he means, Beth's translucent agate bowl appears in the center of the adjoined tables. Under the table, Dandelion meows a soft greeting to Kip. In the next second, Beth appears at the north end of the table and exclaims, "Hey, you two, we were hoping we'd catch you when you got back from your run. How's your week

74

gone? Do you have time for me to tell you about the new Elizabeth Ann I met last week?"

Seeing Liz's excited nod, Beth continues, "She calls herself Ann Anderson. I've gone back to visit her dimension every day since and think we're becoming good friends. Her home sits on the hillside above the cliffs as her Redcliff's Beach as her Dad's cabin was destroyed much as my beach was. Her beach is a rocky mess with a high shoreline..." As Beth tells about Ann and her dimension, Liz listens without interrupting.

Then Beth tell her, "This morning I didn't get to see Ann. Instead, I went to the crystal cave you told me about last week. When the cave entrance opened on the cliff face, I recognized the stairs from what you'd told me and ran up the curving staircase as I knew what to expect..."

When Beth finishes telling her experiences in the crystal room, Liz exclaims, "Beth, I'm so happy that you saw the crystal room. What a wonderful dream you had. I'm so excited for you. Kip and I have gone there every morning this week. I find it interesting that, though we were both there, we didn't see each other."

"Was Kip with you? Dandy was with me, too. I'd think that those two would have seen each other even if we didn't. Their sixth senses are so much better than ours. Dandy's started talking to me. At least, I hear thoughts in my head that must be from her. Is that how Kip talks with you?"

"Yes, that's exactly how he does it. I'm not surprised that Dandy does it too, Kip told me he and Dandy are old friends. We probably have to go to the crystal room together at the same time. Why don't we try that? It would be wonderful to share such an amazing place. Each time we've gone, Kip hurries me to the center of the fire-opal floor. Then he turns in circles as if chasing his tail. If I don't go fast enough, he barks three times until I'm turning at the same tempo he is right in the center of the floor. On today's visit, a song filled my head and I sang it as if I knew it. However, when I left the cave, the song stayed in the crystal room. I couldn't remember a single note outside the cave."

Sitting up, Kip lays his head on Liz's lap and she buries her face into the thick ruffle of fur around his neck. Giving him a hug, she says, "Love you."

Love you most, partner.

Looking up at Beth, Liz says, "I'm not surprised you've met another Parallel Life, Beth. After all, you are the original child. What do you do to make certain that you'll go into Ann's dimension?"

"As I'm running to the cliffs, I think only of her and Honey and as soon as I slap the touchstone and shout our mantra, I'm there. That worked until today. However, I won't complain about going into the crystal room. It was wonderful. Dandy enjoyed it, too."

"Yes, I'm sure she did. Kip told me he's been there many lifetimes. Sometimes, Beth, I'm dumbstruck and in complete awe of this animal. I'm so glad he chose me. I love him so much."

Beth watches Kip stare up at Liz and says, "He's your familiar, just as Dandy is mine. Do you understand about 'familiars'? They are animals who knew us in past lives and come back each lifetime to watch over us. Do you understand what I'm saying?"

"Of course, I don't doubt that one bit. Kip is much more than any ordinary dog. When he came to me, I began to see everything differently. He opened my mind and heart to receive new people and new experiences. The day I first met Dr. Parker, Kip told me he was a good man and I let Dan into our lives." Liz says, "I'm glad to say that both Kip and I are both falling hard for the charming Dr. Parker."

Beth chuckles, "I'm not at all surprised. I told you on the first of the month that new energies would come your way and to give them a chance. I'm so proud of you, Liz. Opening up to new people takes courage. Especially where the question of love is concerned. I like that Kip lets you know if people are good or not, Dandy does the same for me. She keeps me settled within my space. You are so right, she and Kip are friends from another life. Isn't that lovely?"

"Yes, it certainly is. I'd like Eliza to meet Kip and get to know him. Since her sister died, I seldom see her and he'd be so good for her. If you see her today, update her on what's happening. I fear that our connection may be weakening."

Beth smiles, "Don't worry about our connections to each other, Liz. They're solid. Eliza has gotten on a different time schedule then before. She was here earlier and heading into Ocean Shores to take the last of Marie's things to a shop that sells secondhand goods. Seems she's been working there every day and loves it."

As Beth speaks there is a loud rapping at Liz's front door and Kip barks three times before he races to stand in front of it. Instantly Beth's dimension vanishes and Liz follows Kip to the door. When she opens it, she finds Mary Jackson standing there holding her backpack and camera.

Smiling at Liz and Kip, she exclaims, "Hey there neighbors. I was wondering if I could crawl under your deck to photograph a pair of Elegant Terns I've seen flying in and out from under your deck the past several days. If you don't mind, I'd need to photograph their nest and eggs, if there are any. I'm keeping records on as many nesting pairs of terns as I can find and need to photograph them all."

Liz smiles at her fast patter and says, "Of course, go under and do your thing. At least it'll be safer than hanging off cliff ledges. Your dangling last week was way too scary. It looked as if you were in some sort of a thriller movie. When you're done under the deck, if you have time, come in for iced tea and some girl talk. We need time without the guys around."

"That sounds great. Shouldn't be more than an hour or so. Will that work for you?"

"Yes. I'll be in my office writing, so come through the slider and yell. I usually keep it open for Kip. However, if I don't close him inside today, he'll keep you company under the deck. He goes under there several times a day and now I know what he's been checking out. I don't think he's disturbed the nest as those terns don't seem to mind his nosing around, as they keep coming back."

"Let him come with me. I'd like to see how he interacts with the birds. We'll see you in an hour or so."

Two hours later, Mary stamps the sand off her shoes and brushes off her jeans while Kip shakes himself hard before the two enter through the open slider door and Mary shouts, "Hey, Liz, Kip and I are back."

Kip races into Liz's office and pulls at her until she follows him out to the kitchen. By this time, Mary has filled two tall glasses with ice and tea from a pitcher in the fridge and sets them next to a plate of brownies on a tray. Taking the tray from her, Liz says, "Bring the pitcher of tea with you. We'll both want more after the first brownie, they're a bit dry." Then she walks out to the deck and places the tray on the table. Coming behind with the pitcher of tea, Mary joins her and the two women settle into chairs for a long chat.

Mary talks about the pairs of terns Kip pointed out to her under the deck. "I swear, Liz, I don't think I would have seen two of the nests if Kip hadn't shown them to me. They look new and are well hidden along the basalt next to the cabin's foundation. There are three older nests on the cement posts holding the deck off the sand. Those nests look as if they've been used several years as there's quite a pile of stuff under them. It looks pretty storm resistant as the nests look very snug."

"Thanks, I'll check on them this fall. I doubt anyone else has been under those decks until you were today. That means there must be years of their mess. How bad is it other places?"

"Fairly clean except where the newer nests have been build. Did I say there are five nests down there? Kip got me acquainted with each of the pairs. They all seemed not to notice Kip. At least, they weren't frightened off by him. It was only my camera that got them worried. That boy of yours stood guard and I was able to take my shots. He's quite a dog, almost seemed he could talk to them. Yes, I'd say he is quite a dog, aren't you Kip?"

An hour later, Mary thanks Liz for the tea as she swings her pack over her shoulders. As Liz walks her to the front door, she asks, "Would you and Larry come over for dinner tonight? Dan is coming and he enjoys you both so much. It would make the evening very special. Please say you'll come."

Surprised but pleased, Mary exclaims, "Why that would be lovely, Liz. Thank you. What could we bring?"

"Just yourselves. Around six?"

After the door shuts behind Mary, Liz looks at Kip and says, "I like

Mary very much. She's intelligent and interesting, a good combination for a friend. What do you think?"

She's a good person.

Smiling at him, Liz replies, "Yes, she is."

Going into the kitchen, Liz opens the fridge and pulls out a large baking dish with a rump roast sitting in red wine marinade. The aroma causes her mouth to water as if she's sucked a pickle. Moving the roast onto the counter, she covers it with foil and sets it on the middle shelf of the oven. When she sets the temperature and timer, she sees Kip watching her every move, and laughs, "Sorry, Kip, this meat's too pricey and too spicy. How'd you like a nice knuckle bone? Would that make you happy? Do you want it now?"

Yes. Yes. Yes.

When it's nearly five thirty, Kip barks three times, races to the front door and waits impatiently for Liz to open it. When she does, he races down the entry deck to the front of the garage and she sees a sleek red car snaking through the trees along the driveway. After it stops in front of the garage, the dog spins with excitement until the car door opens and Dr. Dan Parker gets out. The man claps his hands twice and Kip leaps into his arms. The dog's momentum sends the man spinning on his heels as if a he were running for the goal line.

Delighted by the connection between her two males, Liz feels very lucky to have both of them in her life. When the dog pushes out of his arms, Dan turns a radiant face to Liz, who says, "Greetings, Dr. Dan. I'm so glad you didn't end up on the tarmac just then. That was a very fancy catch."

"Kip's a great dog. We're going to be great friends. All of us." Dan says as he comes up to Liz.

Backing away, Liz turns towards the door and says, "I'm glad you're earlier than planned as Mary and Larry are joining us for dinner tonight. Mary came over this afternoon to photograph Elegant Terns that have nests under my beach side deck. Then the two of us had a long chat. I enjoyed her so much so I asked if she and Larry could come for dinner. They'll be here around six."

As she talks, Dan tussles with Kip and lets the dog lay wet kisses over his face. Wiping them off the best he can, Dan grabs Liz's arm and spins her around to face him. Then pokes his face down to hers and says. "How about a big wet kiss from you, too, sweetie? Kip's made sure my face is clean."

Ducking away from his hold, Liz laughs a bit uncomfortably as she hurries through the open front door, "Not with Kip's slobber all over it, you silly. Go wash, then we'll talk about kisses. I don't know why you let Kip do that. He eats all sorts of strange things from off the beach… ICK… Get away, doggy breath."

Laughing loudly, Dan claps his hands again and Kip runs out the open slider door to the beach deck. A few seconds later, the dog returns with a yellow tennis ball in his mouth. Dropping it at Dan's feet, the dog dances away. When Parker picks up the ball, Kip runs towards the beach and the ball sails over the dog's head. Racing after it, the delighted animal catches it on the second bounce and trots back to the slider door. Then Kip lies down on the doormat, with the ball in his mouth and looks at the two people standing next to the kitchen counter.

Once he threw the ball, Dan disappeared into the powder room to wash his face. As Kip watches, Dan is nuzzling Liz's neck and ear lobes causing her to giggle. Then he turns her to face him and he plants a full mouthed kiss on her lips. When they come up for air, he asks, "When are the Jacksons due?"

"Too soon for what you have in mind. Now, get out of here, you brute."

"Mm. Mm, you smell good enough to eat. What perfume is that you're wearing?"

"It's called Eau-de-vino-de-spices-eau-garlic and you smell it because it's on the roast that's in the oven. So glad you like it." Liz chuckles. "This chef aims to please in all things sensual. Oh-oh, your friend is staring at you from the doorway and has the yellow ball in his mouth. Why don't you two go to the beach and de-stress until the Jacksons get here? I'll have Larry walk down and get you."

"Sounds like a good idea. What do you say, Kip?" Dan asks the dog now bouncing in the open doorway, his golden eyes flashing as he squishes the yellow tennis ball in his mouth.

After a long friendly dinner, Liz loads the dishwasher while Mary makes a pitcher of Sangria, fills tall glasses with ice and carries it out to the deck table and chairs where the two men are seated. Close behind her, Liz follows with a platter of fruits and cheeses. At the women's approach, both men get up to help and the women let them take over. Soon the air is filled with laughter and chatter as the friends share antidotes of their lives. When the sunset begins to fade, there is a lull in the conversation as each watches the day come to a close.

Sitting in the moonlight, the mood changes and Larry Jackson clears his throat then says, "Liz? Could I ask you about those runs you do each morning?"

"Sure, Larry, what is it you want to know?"

"How long have you been doing them?"

"Actually they were started by my parents when my sister Dana and I were tiny babies. My Dad had discovered the golden stone in the cliff face when he was building the cabin. Right after that a hunk of the stone fell off the one in the cliff and he caught it with his hands. Then he placed that hunk of golden agate under the dining table where it still is. Every day after he took our family to the beach, he would walk us up to the cliffs and we all slap the golden agate in the cliff face and shout. 'I declare this run good and done.'

"As we grew, my sister and I raced each other to be the first to slap the touchstone. When we got into our teens, it didn't matter who got there first, just that we slapped the stone together and that's what we did, every morning. In fact, it was the last thing we did together as a family, here at the beach, before we left for home. It turned out to be the last day I had a family. On the way back to Portland, we were in a horrible car wreck and my parents and sister, Dana Marie, were all killed. I've never forgotten a moment of being with them that last day and I run in their memory, treasuring every second of it."

Hearing the sadness in her voice, Larry says, "I'm sorry my question made you sad, Liz. If you don't want to say anything more, don't. I don't need to know any more."

"No, go ahead and ask, Larry. I've no secrets and your all good friends."

"Okay, then, here goes. I've been watching your run to the cliffs each morning for about a month. You ran at the same time I eat my breakfast and see you out that window next to the table. A couple weeks ago, after Kip came into your life, something happened that startled me. It began a week ago."

Tipping her head, Liz looks into his eyes and asks, "Whatever could startle you about my running up the beach with Kip?"

"It isn't while you and Kip are running, Liz. It's what happens right after you slap that stone in the cliff face. I first saw it about a week ago. You slapped the stone and disappeared. Vanished into thin air. The first time, I thought my eyes were tricking me. After that, I watched your run every morning and it has happened each time. Just to make sure I wasn't going crazy, a couple days ago, I asked Mary to watch with me. The first time she saw you two vanish, she became hysterical and wanted me to call 911. I assured her that you both would return to the beach within two hours. Sure enough, two hours later you and Kip came running down the beach as if nothing had happened. She only relaxed when you ran onto your deck. Are we crazy or what?"

For nearly a minute, Liz looks from Larry to Mary to Dan and back again, silently questioning Kip, *Should I tell them the truth, Kip? Should I tell them who we really are? Will they understand? Will Dan?*

Now is better than later. Dan needs to show his true self.

Kip's answer surprises Liz and she frowns at him. Sighing, she turns to Larry and says, "I don't know why I owe you an explanation, Larry. However, I do feel it's time Dan knows the truth about who I really am. Before I begin, I want you each to understand that what I'm going to tell you is the absolute truth, as I know it. What I tell you tonight is neither from my imagination nor is it a type of hysteria. It is what has happened to me over the last year, right up to this moment."

When Liz begins to talk, the three people she considers good friends fall silent and watch her closely as she speaks of losing her husband, Peter; of his secret life; of Alex Petrow's broken friendship; of meeting her Parallel Lives, Beth Anderson and Eliza Staples. Then she tells how Kip came to her at the touchstone, how he took her into the cave to the crystal room and what happens whenever they are inside it. Finally, she tells of how Kip and Dandelion are the animal familiars to herself and Beth.

As she speaks, Liz watches each face in front of her. Larry's face is wide with interest and acceptance. Mary's seems awed with wonder. However, it is the face of Dr. Dan Parker that shows nothing, not a reaction nor an emotion. The man who opened her heart to love again, simply stares at her with a blank face that shouts louder than any words could. In those moments, Liz understands without a doubt that Dr. Dan Parker has fled from her life.

However, his blank face fills her with a determination to fully explain the events of the past year, so Liz takes all the time she needs. When everything is said, Liz gives each person a long questioning look, then says, "That's all I have to say about my life. There is nothing more to tell, take it or leave it."

Heaving a sigh of relief, Liz sips the last of the Sangria in her glass and relaxes into the comfort of the high backed deck chair. Their silence makes it seem as if the three have fallen into a trance. Wishing for the evening to be over, Liz barks, "For heavens sakes, Larry, you wanted the truth about my runs and I told you. If you have trouble accepting what I've said, go home and sleep on it. Set it aside for as long as you need. If you want, I'll talk with you again. I leave it up to each of you to tell me how you see me in your future."

Dan Parker's silence screams the loudest and when she reaches for his hand, he jerks it away. Staring at his blank face, Liz knows that without a doubt there is nothing left for her from this handsome veterinarian and she stands up. "Well, I'm calling it a night. Come, Kip, let's go to bed. I've had enough of baring my soul. To hell with you all."

"Wait, don't leave us." Mary exclaims, "My, gosh, gal, give us time to react. What you've told us about your past year has thrown me for a loop. What a terrible time you went through with Peter's death, then the attack by your best friend and when those Parallel Lives appeared within your home, it must have been horrible to say the least. It all seems too much for any one person and still keep sane. I guess I'd like to know how you tell one Parallel Life from the other if they look exactly the same as you do. How can you tell one from the other?"

Relieved that someone has asked a question that she can answer, Liz sits back down and says, "At first it was difficult, as we're the same person in every way. However, I've come to realize that we each have different lifestyles, desires, hairstyles, clothing, even our speech patterns are different. Of course, our daily choices bring out the most pronounced differences."

Suddenly irritated by the men's silence, Liz turns to Larry Jackson and snaps, "Well, Mr. Jackson? I've just bared my soul to so that you can understand what you saw while staring at me running every morning, say something. I told you that I have nothing more to add to it. Take it or leave it. One more thing you should know, we Elizabeth Ann Andersons have come to the conclusion that Beth Anderson is the original child. How we came to realize this is nobody's business. We know it to be true."

Larry shifts uncomfortably in his seat and Liz sees he is staring at Dan and waiting for the man's reaction, just as she is. Then he turns to Liz and says, "Thank you, Liz. I'm sorry I didn't speak right away. You answered my questions more completely than I ever expected. It definitely explains what I saw happen. Thanks for sharing so much with us. I'm so relieved to find out that I saw what I saw. I'm positive you told us the truth as you lived it. I don't see how anyone could possibly doubt you. What do you have to say, Dan? Didn't I tell you that Liz was a special person? What do you think about your lovely lady now?"

When Dan does not speak, Liz says to him, "I'd hoped each of you would listen with an open mind and that you'd accept who I am. I can tell from your expression, Dan, that you haven't. It's your loss, Dan. Go away and find some normal lady friend. I am who I said and I won't change for you or anyone else."

After she speaks, the three watch Dr. Parker and wait for him to speak. Several minutes of silence pass when the stoic man picks up his glass, drinks the last sip of liquid, sets the empty glass on the tray in the center of the table and stands. Louder than any shout, Dr. Dan Parker walks silently into the cabin, picks his jacket off the sofa, goes out the front door and closes it softly behind him. In the seconds that follow, the three on the deck hear the car's motor starting, tires crunching on gravel and a powerful engine gaining momentum on Shoreline Drive.

It's then that Liz breaks the silence. "And that is Dr. Dan Parker's answer. Good riddance I say. I'll never be bothered by him ever again. I'm sorry for you, Kip as I know you enjoyed him. Didn't you know his answer would be this way?"

I said it was time for Dan Parker to show his true self, didn't I?

EIGHT

June 10th—Beth

BETH is determined to return to Ann Anderson's dimension this morning. As she runs, she remembers that first rather frightening encounter with this other Elizabeth Ann at the top the cliffs in another dimension. Since that time, Beth has gone back to that dimension several times and the two of them have become comfortable with each other. Besides, their animal familiars, Dandelion and Honey, have told them they've known each other many lifetimes. Though the two women laughed at that idea, they both feel certain it is true.

Slapping the touchstone, Beth is confident that they will be in Ann's dimension as soon as she shouts, "I declare this run good and done." And she's pleased when the dimension changes and the touchstone moves from the cliff face to create a stairway down to the rocky beach as it has before. However, when she turns to wave to Ann where she always waits on the shoreline, she is nowhere in sight. Turning back to the cliff face, Beth sees it has a wide arched opening through which a brightly lit stairwell rising up into a cave within the cliffs.

Staring at the stairs, Beth shouts, "My God, Dandy, this has to be the staircase Liz told us about, the one that goes up to a giant geode. Come on, Dandy, let's go see that crystal room. Look, the light moves across the ceiling and walls of the stairs just as Liz said it did for her."

Dashing through the cave's entrance, the large orange cat leads Beth up the stairs. Amazed how the stairs wrap around the basalt flow, Beth runs to the top of the stairs. There she finds Dandy sitting in the middle of a wide hallway, cleaning her paws, and looking at her with come-hither eyes. Beth laughs, 'Oh Dandy, you are such a prima donna."

Leaping straight in the air, Dandelion meows and dashes into an alcove on the left side of the hall where she jumps from a marble bundle to marble bundle held on the shoulders of exquisitely carved marble statues of a totally nude men. Even though, Liz has described these statues to her, Beth is startled when the stone sculpted humanlike forms seem to move.

Running to the end of the hallway, Beth turns to call Dandy and realizes it is the moving lights that causes the statues to seem alive. Chuckling at her own unease, Beth picks Dandy up in her arms before continuing around the end wall and sees the wide opening of the giant geode Liz had told her was there. The rounded edge of the opening is covered with masses of tiny crystals, each flashing so brightly that she has to squint in order to see anything against the glare.

Even though Liz had described the phenomenon so perfectly, Beth is stunned by its beauty of the natural opening. Running her hands over the tiny crystals covering the edges of the wide opening, she exclaims, "Look, Dandy. See how perfectly these tiny groups of crystals lay into and over each other. Liz was so right, this place is amazing. How wonderful."

Touching the tiny tips of the crystals, Beth whispers, "There must be thousands upon thousands upon thousands of these tiny crystals all over the surface of this opening. Liz was right, this is a giant geode. Just look at the size of that room beyond and the crystals hanging everywhere. Even the mass of this huge crystal formation blocking our way is perfection. This geode must have formed millions of years ago when the lava flows were cooling in seawater. It's as if it has been molded by the hand of God."

Looking past the huge crystal, Beth stares up at the opening in the cave's ceiling. "There, that's the hole in the ceiling that lets sunlight inside. Liz said to look for a path into that room at the bottom of that last facet. We should see a path of fire-opal tiles to follow into the room. Can you see the path, Dandy?"

With a loud meow, Dandelion trots past the last facet and disappears. Startled, Beth calls out, "Wait, Dandy, where did you go?"

Instantly, the cat's head pops out from behind the bottom of the facet. "Meow-rrr?" the animal questions her and again disappears. Hurrying to slip between the facet and the granite wall of the cliffs, Beth sees a faint glow on the floor and follows the path until it blends into a wide circular floor. At the same time, Dandy scampers out through openings between larger crystal formations and says, "Meow-wwrr?" before she dashes behind another group of crystals.

"Good girl, you found me, now stay close to me."

As Beth reaches the edge of the path, the cat scampers past her and scampers across the fire-opal tiles to the center of the wide circular floor. At that moment, sunlight again fills the room. Immediately, Dandelion hops up and down on the tiles as if her feet were on fire. Laughing with delight, Beth watches the cat leap from lighted tile to lighted tile trying to catch the colors moving within the fire-opal tiles. Finally, the lights dim and the cat comes back to Beth with a questioning, "Meow-rrr?"

Reaching down, Beth picks the animal up and says, "Those fire-opals only look as if they're on fire, Dandy, but aren't they beautiful?"

In that instant, sunlight again fills the crystal room and the two are covered with brilliant flashing lights as each facet rebounds the light across the room touching of thousands upon thousands of facets that flash light back and forth to masses of crystal groupings around the massive space. Turning her back to the rebounding sunlight, she walks to the dimmer side of the room.

From there, Beth and Dandy watch the lights rebound from crystal facet to crystal facet to crystal facet, flashing back and forth through the room. "How exciting, Dandy. Look at the change the sunlight made in the room. What an exquisite space. Whenever sunlight comes through that hole in the ceiling, the light hits the facets that hit everything else. Just look at the colors in those tiles when the light hits them. No wonder you thought those fire-opals were on fire. It's easy to see why those precious gems were used as tiles on the floor. I think we are very lucky to come here when clouds dim the light off and on. Liz said sun was so bright when she came that she had to put a scarf over her eyes while she was in here.

"We're seeing more of this amazing cave than she did just because the light dims now and then. I'll have to tell her about these things we see which she didn't talk about. Wow, here's the sun again. Look how those facets flash back and forth. Doesn't it look magical, Dandy? And the flashing is only caused by the refracted light. What an amazing display."

Looking down at Dandy to give her eyes a rest, Beth remembers what Liz said about turning in the center of the room and of hearing a song and asks the cat, "Should we turn in the center of the room? Liz said she heard music when she did that was beautiful."

As if in answer to her question, Dandy touches her neck with one paw and purrs loudly. Amazed by the cat's reaction, Beth goes to the center of the fire-opal tiled floor and begins to turn. She closed her eyes only when sunlight fills the room and the lights flash. Soon, it is apparent to Beth that some highly intelligent group of people discovered the crystal room, carved the steps into the room and laid the fire-opal tiles. She becomes certain that this beautiful room has been used for centuries and more information is shown to her with each of her turns.

When deep peaceful calm comes over Beth, a wondrous tune fills her mind and the sweet song flows from her throat. As her voice fills the cave, the crystals begin to vibrate and Dandy puts one paw to Beth's throat as if to feel the vibrations of the music. The louder Beth sings, the faster she turns and soon the colors in the floor blend together as if embers from a wildfire have been spread across the room and are left to burn out. Looking across the glowing tiles to the far side of the room, she sees the bench carved from the stone in the cliffs. Then, she's how it runs the length of the room and ends at a set of stairs that climb up the wall to the opening in the cave's ceiling.

As she stares at the opening, sunlight again fills the room and Beth closes her eyes against the brilliant light. At this time, she is compelled to turn faster and faster twirling as fast as she can. Purring loudly, the cat wraps her paws around Beth's neck and snuggles in place on Beth's shoulders. Now, with her hands no longer holding Dandy, she spreads her arms out to the sides and spins, letting the words of the song pour from her mouth. Though the words are in a language she does not know she understands their full meaning.

As the music begins to keep tempo with the flashes of the lights and Beth falls into a deep trance. When this happens, she lifts off the floor and is laid upon the fire-opal tiles.

At that moment, Dandelion purrs so loudly that Beth awakens to find she is seated upon a large platform covered with a brightly colored mattress and dozens of pillows of various sizes. This platform is secured in the center of a seagoing longboat that is propelled by two dozen strong men pulling on long oars that force the craft across a wide azure sea and she knows only these things for certain:

She knows she was chosen because of her extreme beauty, her purity and her true kindness.

She knows she is to leave her home planet and travel through the wormholes to some unknown place in order to save her planet and its peoples.

She knows the beautiful longboat was built to take her on this trip and that it will return laden with riches, but without her and her orange cat.

She knows she will never see her loving family again.

She knows she will be joined in marriage to a handsome young man from U-ran-o-sis, a planet far from Earth.

As she looks around the longboat, she sees how highly decorated it is, both inside and out, with the most intricate of designs which are edged with gold. The bow of the longboat has a massive carved dragon's head with smoke puffing out from its nostrils. Flapping slowly at the sides of the craft, are two huge wooden wings, powered by strong men inside the boat, each rising and lowering as the ship moves across the ocean. At the stern of the longboat, extending far behind, is a long pointed dragon's tail with many colorful flags attached to it that wave to the hundred longboats following behind.

When her elegant longboat enters a wide deep bay, the oarsmen rest their oars and the helmsman guides the boat with the rudder so the longboat glides, as if by magic, across the calm waters. As the ship comes towards a huge granite slab at the base of high red granite cliffs, it turns broadside to the slab and gently taps the edge of this landing. The beauty sees this granite pier is decorated with the same colorful flags and banners which are on the longboat and that many more banners of various colors go from the pier to the top of the cliff face.

Holding her bold orange cat close to her breasts, the beauty braces herself in order to jump onto the landing if need be. However, the rocking boat calmly settles beside the moorage and six of the oarsmen step onto the granite moorage to secure the boat with thick ropes. A moment later, an elegant young man appears from an opening in the cliff face and approaches the longboat, smiling directly at the young beauty.

This young man wears wondrous robes of red silks and spun gold which he swishes to the side as he springs into the longboat to stand at the end of the platform where the beauty is seated holding her cat. Beaming down at her, the young man bows low and says, "Greetings and good fortune to you, lovely Elizabeth Ann of Earth. I am you intended, Rurik of U-ran-o-sis. Come. Rise up. Stand beside me. For on this day you and I are to be united. Our futures await."

At that, the young man reaches out his hand to Elizabeth of Earth who grasps it and allows him to pull her onto her feet. Then the two young people step out of the boat onto the granite moorage. Lifting her hand to his lips, Rurik of U-ran-o-sis presses his lips to it and, during these few seconds, he assesses both her physical beauty and the exquisite jewels adorning her. Young Rurik's eyes blaze with triumph and he whispers, "Follow me, Elizabeth Ann of Earth, we will walk the path of knowledge and share eternity together."

Hearing the excitement in his voice, the young beauty smiles with the pleasure of knowing both her beauty and her jewels may be the rarest of all things, but it is her virginity that is her golden key to this royal life. Then the handsome Rurik leads her across the granite and they bow to the multitude of people amassed along the shoreline. When the teeming crowd sees this, the people cheer and burst into a song which Elizabeth Ann of Earth has known from childhood. Touched by so much love, the young beauty sings full voiced with them and, when the song is finished, she bows to show her love for the people and the masses cheer.

At that time, young Rurik of U-ran-o-sis leads the beautiful Elizabeth Ann of Earth to the high arched entrance in the cliff face. Looking up at the large golden stone set in the high point of the arch, both reach up to slap it hard and shout, "I declare this run good and done."

Again, the masses cheer and the young couple turn to bow again. Then, the young Rurik of U-ran-o-sis pulls the young beauty in through the opening and up the winding staircase until they reach a wide hallway. Here, the beauty sets her bold cat onto the whitest marble floor she has ever seen and hurries after the handsome man to where he stands, in front of two alcoves, halfway down the hallway. When he steps into the alcove on the left, the young man bows low to each statue of a nude male. Seeing him do this, the young beauty does the same.

Then he takes her hands and shows her how to play her hands over the statues' genitals. At first, she blushes and pulls away. However, when Rurik insists she does as he asks, the young beauty runs her hands over each of the statues. When she is finished, the young man leads the blushing beauty across the hallway and they bow to the three female marble statues in that alcove. This time, Rurik of U-ran-o-sis boldly steps up to each statue and playfully moves his hands over every inch of the naked female forms.

When this is done, the young man takes the young woman in his arms and presses his body to hers, holding her in an intimate embrace for several seconds. This time, his kiss is open mouthed and his tongue probes into hers. Though, he holds her with great gentleness, the young beauty pushes away from the young man's arms and Rurik of U-ran-o-sis can see that Elizabeth Ann of Earth has a dazed look.

Quickly leading her to the end of the hallway where the wall curves out of sight, the young man pulls the young beauty into his arms again and kisses her passionately, moving his hands over her body as he did the marble statues. Responding with her own passion, the beauty pushes her body against his and feels his large growth move against her. Unable to do otherwise, she spreads her legs wide and Rurik of U-ran-o-sis reaches to lift her up to him.

At the moment of his intimate touch, the beauty pushes away with great force as she remembers she must hold onto her highest value until all of the rites have been performed, for without the purest gift of her golden virginity, she be unfit to marry into this royal family.

Standing away from him, the young beauty holds her chin high as she arranges her clothing and shows her resolve without looking at the young man Seeing this, the young man knows that he must control his urges until the rites have been performed or he will shame his planet, his people and his elders who have raised him to stand above all others.

When the orange cat meows loudly, she looks down at where it sits next to her feet. Smiling at the animal, the young beauty lifts it up and, holding it between her breasts, looks at the young man with a radiant smile which tells him of the many wondrous things that will come to him. Beaming back at her, the young man bows to show his admiration of her strengths.

Continuing around the curved wall, the young lovers stop in front of the opening of a giant geode where a massive crystal room can be seen. There, ten boys and ten girls carefully drape brightly colored silk scarves over each of the couple's head. When this is done, the children lead them down a path of glowing fire-opal tiles, to a crowd of people filling the massive room. Each of these people holds a tall golden staff and when the young couple bow to them, the crowd raises these staffs high over their heads and cheer wildly.

Then the ten children lead the pair across the wide floor of the crystal room and leave them in front of a wall of azure colored crystals in which two exquisite thrones, encrusted with jewels, await for them. Turning to face the center of the wide room, Rurik of U-ran-o-sis and Elizabeth Ann of Earth bow to show their love and humility to those within the crystal room. Again, this crowd of people raise their staffs high over their heads and cheer.

Then the handsome young man stands before the beauty and kisses both her cheeks. Then she kisses his lips and the cheers for as long as she holds her lips to his. When the two part, both their faces are flushed bright pink and the young man leads the blushing beauty up the stairs to the first crystal throne and she sits. Before he releases her hand, he kisses the beauty on the lips for a full minute and bows low to her. Again, the crystal room explodes with cheers and the young beauty releases her orange cat to her lap where it snuggles down for a much needed nap.

As the young man stands beside the second throne, he points up to the opening in the ceiling of the crystal room and the onlookers turn to watch what he sees. There, entering from the opening, is an exquisitely handsome older couple who slowly descend the stairs. Each of these older people wears robes of the riches reds silks with threads of spun gold and each holds a long staff of pure gold topped with a large globe encrusted with jewels of all sorts. As the couple come down the stairwell, the masses of people, both inside and outside, roar their approval.

When the elegant couple steps onto the fire-opal tiles, they cross the floor and stop in front of the young couple seated on the high thrones. Without a moment of hesitation, the handsome older man raises his golden staff with both hands and holds there for a full minute. Then, as the crowd continues to cheer, he holds it over the younger man's outstretched hands and the youth takes it from his elder's hands. Immediately, the youth raises the staff high over his own head for a full minute, then he places it so that it stands upright, next to his left foot. All the while the elder and the youth show their respect and love for each other, the masses of people cheer.

Letting the roar subside, the older man reaches above his head and lifts off his crown of spun gold imbedded with large emeralds and rubies. Stepping away from the crystal thrones, he raises the crown over his head and turns to face all sides of the crystal room. After a full minute, he steps close to the front of the crystal throne and carefully places the glittering crown upon the youth's bowed head. When this is done, the older man steps back and bows very low to the young man, acknowledging the fact that young Rurik of U-ran-o-sis has been crowned the new King of all he surveys. Again, the crowd goes wild with excitement.

Then, the elegant older woman steps forward and bows to the young man, lifts her golden staff over his jeweled crown and taps it three times with the encrusted jeweled globe. Again, the multitude of onlookers cheer the newly crowned King and the young beauty beside him reaches out one jeweled hand to the young King and he presses it to his lips. In return, the young beauty brings his hand to her lips and kisses his palm.

Unable to control himself, the young man gasps loudly with emotion and the beauty is pleased to see the flare of passion in his eyes. When the masses see the intense connection between the young couple, there is such a great roar within the massive room that the crystals begin to peel as if bells. It is during this moment that the young beauty sees all those within the cave, young and old, have thick white hair and eyes of azure blue, just as she and the royal family have.

A sharp rapping brings the cheering to an end and all faces turn to watch the older Queen raise her long golden staff, with its large jeweled golden globe, high over her head. Turning to face all sides of the room, the elder woman rotates the staff so the jewels on the encrusted globe flash their colors throughout the crystal room. At that time, the young beauty sees that those splendid jewels rival those which she wears. When the Queen is certain every eye is upon her, she bows very low to young Elizabeth Ann of Earth.

Instantly, the multitude of people, both inside and outside the crystal room, erupt into the song which the young beauty knows well.

Standing at her throne, Elizabeth Ann of Earth spreads her arms wide, as if to embrace the Queen and her people, and sings full voiced with the rousing crowd.

When the song is finished, the elegant older woman steps close to the young beauty's crystal throne and holds the long golden staff up with both hands. Looking into the young beauty's eyes, the older woman carefully lays the long jeweled encrusted staff into the beauty's outreached hands and bows very low.

Knowing to hold the staff and raise it high over her own head, the young beauty holds it there for a full minute as the masses cheer. It is then the young beauty realizes she is now the Queen of U-ran-o-sis and she smiles down at the older woman who nods with pleasure.

In that instant, Beth awakens from her trance to find she is lying flat on her back in the center of the fire-opal tiled floor and that Dandy is curled up on top of her lap purring loudly. Beth strokes the animal's soft fur as her mind slowly returns from the intense dream.

It is then that a vision of all people who have been a part of her life comes before Beth. One at a time, they state their case and Beth remembers how she treated them or how they treated her. To those who treated her badly, she forgives. To those she treated badly she asks forgiveness. To those who were generous and good to her, she thanks with deepest gratitude. To those who are to come in the future, she welcomes with love and good wishes.

As she reviews the consequences of these actions, she asks forgiveness for her transgressions. When the vision vanishes, Beth feels an inner peace which she has never known before. All the negatives she has held during her life, past and present, are released and she heals in ways she will never fully understand or be able to explain, even to herself.

As she sits up, Dandy leaps onto the fire-opal tiles and runs towards the stairs up to the opening in the cave's ceiling. Smiling at the cat's decision, Beth knows it is time to leave for home and follows the animal up the stairs. Ascending the steps, Beth wonders which dimension will be on the outside of the opening, her own or Ann's. When she sees, Dandelion disappear out the opening, she smiles as she knows the cat would not lead her into danger.

When Beth steps into the sunshine, she sees Dandelion waiting within tall seagrasses covering a high earthen berm which encircles the opening, hiding it from the outside. As Beth reaches the top of the berm, she looks down and sees Ann Anderson squatting in front of the stone fireplace. Beth yells, "Hey, Ann, I'm up here. Which way should I came down there?"

Spinning around, Ann looks up and shouts, "Beth? What... What a fright you gave me. Oh? I see... you came out the crystal room. I wondered if you would come here this morning. Is Dandelion with you? Of course, there she is."

Then, pointing to the right, Ann says, "Go that way. There's a zig-zagging path down to the wall. Yeah, that's it. Good. Did you enjoy the crystal room? It's amazing, isn't it?"

"Yes, it is." Beth answers as she leaves the path and stops next to Ann still poking at a fire in the fireplace. "It was the first time I've been in there. Liz found it a week ago and has come back several times since. This morning I was trying to come back here, but after I slapped my touchstone, the entrance to the crystal room opened. Funny how that happened. I was thinking of you and went in there instead. I didn't linger at the alcoves' statues, as Liz said I could see them another time. I went directly into the crystal room as she suggested. She was so right. It was wonderful. I was stunned by the formations and colors in there. Do you go down there often?"

Smiling, Ann doesn't answer but points down the shoreline and says, "Since you're here now, why don't we go see Dad's floor? I've built a bridge between the sea stacks and I'd like you to show me how you sit at the golden stone in that cement piece. I'm hoping this stone is the same as the one in your floor."

"Will that fire be okay to leave unattended?" Beth asks.

"Oh, yes. I closed down the flue as I'm making coals out of green wood to grill a sea-bass I caught this morning. Can you stay for dinner tonight?" Ann asks Beth. Then, she calls out, "Honey. Come, Honey, Dandy's here. We're going to the sea stacks."

A moment later, the large blond dog bounds from the woods and joyously greets Beth and Dandy. "Hey, Honey, how's my big girl? You and Dandy run ahead. Ann and I'll catch up with you at the end of the trail."

"I want to show off what I've done to Dad's floor. It took a week of scouring to get the grime off the cement and the golden stone. Now it glows so brightly I can now see it from my deck during the day. It's especially bright at night. I want to be sure it's the same as yours before I try to go through to the adjoined tables."

"I'll help any way I can. Do you have any plans about getting your shelter started? It can be much smaller than the original cabin, as you don't plan to live in it, do you?"

"No, I've decided it mainly needs to be strong enough to hold up against whatever storms come at it. I've a rough idea of what I want. Mostly a strong building over the area with the stone. The rest can stay as an open porch. Do you know if there are any plans of Dad's cabin still around?"

"Yes, there are. When Liz did expanded hers, she found a set of Dad's plans in the archives of the Main Library in Portland. She bought a copy, had them framed and now has them hung over her fireplace. I'm sure when you come through at the adjoined tables, she'll let you look at them. Better yet, you might find the same plans at the Portland Library in your own dimension. Those plans show how much thought Dad and Mom put into the cabin and how much loved their family. We Elizabeth Anns were very lucky children to have such wonderful parents."

The two animals run far ahead of the chatting women, as they all follow the trail along the high rough coastline. Intrigued by the extreme difference of Ann's coastline to her own, Beth doesn't notice how far they've walked and is surprised when Ann stops and says, "Here we are, Beth. That bit of path going down through those trees is the last piece of the driveway Dad built to his cabin and those metal legs over to the left are what's left of the old water tank."

Staring at the remains of the old tank as she passes it, Beth follows Ann down the path through the trees. When they're out in the open again, she sees only a wide swath of bare basalt rock dropping off the shoreline. Beth frowns trying to imagine where her own cabin would be sitting. Then she looks out to the three low sea stacks and sees the flat area on the furthest one and whispers, "Dear God, my cabin would be sitting out there."

For several seconds, Beth stares at the level cement area her Dad had poured so many years ago and is dumbfounded that it has held up against the ocean's forces. It takes Ann's shout, from the end of the basalt flow, for Beth move down the rugged slope. Seeing Beth's hesitation, Ann shouts, "Watch your footing, Beth. It's steeper than it looks."

As Beth works her way down to the edge of the shoreline, the gaps between each of the basalt formations seem to get wider than she'd thought they were when she'd stood at the top of the cliffs. Stopping beside Ann, Beth sees that the first gap is nearly twelve feet wide, the second gap a mere five feet and the gap over to the flat basalt stack is twenty feet or wider. More frightening than the spaces is the drop down to the beach below that is nothing but leftover basalt from the sea stacks.

To Beth's surprise, Ann has bridged across each of the gaps using drift logs of all sizes. These are wedged into place and secured to the sea stacks with heavy wire. "Holy cow, Ann, how did you lift those by yourself? Why didn't you wait? I could have helped you?"

"I didn't lift them by myself. Years ago, Dad taught me how to use a 'come-along' winch to haul drift logs into shore to cut up for firewood. I just used that same devise and dragged the logs up the beach. When the tide was high, I'd winch them into position as much as possible. Using the winch made them easy to move and handle them into place. Eventually, I'll lay planking over the logs, but for now this is the footbridge. Use it as if you're crossing a stream on a fallen log and take your time."

Beth says, "My god, Ann, except for that flat floor area on the far basalt stack, I would never believe this is the same spot where my cabin sits today. This is one mean looking beach/"

Beth stares at the debris ten feet below and starts to back away. It's Honey's bark that catches her attentions and she sees that both the dog and the cat have crossed the bridges and are standing on the flat cement. Behind them, she sees the glow of the large agate stone shining brilliantly in the sunlight. Suddenly excited to get over there, Beth starts to pass Ann at the opening onto the first bridge.

Stopping Beth with her arm, Ann exclaims, "Wait here till I get across, Beth. There was a storm last night and I'd like to go over them before you do and check for any loose logs."

Beth laughs, "Good lord, Ann, you used so much bailing wire it'd take a tank to pull those logs down."

"I hope you're right. Still, please wait until I tell you to come. Okay?"

Turning, Ann moves slowly across each bridge checking log. When she reaches the last stack with the smooth cement floor, the animals greet her and she gives both a quick hug. Turning to call Beth over, she shouts, "Okay, Beth, you can come...."

When Beth walks off the last bridge and Ann frowns, saying, "Well, so much for telling you what to do. I guess we really are the same child."

Beth laughs and gives her a hug, "Those logs are tied down with so much wire that these sea stacks will go before the logs fall off. In fact, I'll bet you that you bridges will stay unchanged for the next twenty years, no matter what storms come at you. You build great bridges, kiddo."

It's then that Beth sees the two animals have laid next to the golden stone and she goes to sit beside them. Looking into the stone's glow, Beth sees the same flaws as the stone in her home has and says, "Ann, come and sit by me. I want to show you how I know this is the same as the stone in my home. I think you should build your shelter here as fast as you can. Then you can put a table and chair out here and join Liz, Eliza and me at our adjoined tables."

Sitting down next to Beth, Ann pets Honey and says, "The first time I came to see if the stone was still here, it was covered with seaweeds and barnacles. I began scrubbing it that day and it took a couple days before I got all the debris off. It was as if I had to prove myself to the damn stone before it finally let go of the last hard bits of barnacles. Dirty as it was, it was quite a thrill when I touched the stone's surface. It was then that I knew what you meant about your stone having strong powers. As soon as I cleaned off the stone, I began building the bridges and planning what sort of shelter I could afford."

"Have you sat at the stone yet?" Beth asks.

"Oh yes. Only once though, as I stupidly sat right on top of it. Instantly, a strong surge of energy knocked me off and over backwards. That frightened me so much I've never touched it again except to keep it scrubbed clean. Has your stone ever done that to you or the others?"

Beth laughs, "I told you the stone has strong energy. Last year, when I was shot by my sister, Dee, Liz found me in our adjoined area. I was bleeding badly and she dragged me to the stone and laid me across it. Liz said later that as she watched, I healed from the inside out and that it was the most amazing thing she'd ever seen. We talked about using it again whenever one of us got hurt or fell ill. However, we've all been so healthy this past year the stone was never tested again.

"The touchstone on the cliffs does hold onto my hand until it's given all I am to know. The one like this in my floor never has done that. The three of us believe it's because we played around it when we were children and got used to each other's energy."

Ann exclaims, "I did that, too, when I was a child. Dana Marie and I were always under the table with our dogs and cats. Maybe this one was angry at being ignored these past several years. Show me what you do and I'll do the same. Okay?"

"Okay. Don't be frightened by what happened that first time, Ann. The more you interact with the stone, the gentler it should be with you. After all, you are Elizabeth Ann Anderson."

Ann asks, "How often do you sit at your stone and what part of your body touches it?"

Beth smiles, "I run to the north cliffs every morning to slap the touchstone on the cliff face and listen for messages there. Then, I run back home, clean the sand off my and sit on my chair at the south end of my table. During my meditations, the only part of me that touches the stone are my bare feet. Dandy is usually curled up on top of it by the time I sit, so I tuck my toes under her and meditate on whatever the touchstone told me. Do you want to give it a try and see what happens?"

"Yes, I'd like to try again. Let me sit across from you and watch what you do. Oh dear, Honey's curling up on the stone. She's been doing that as soon as the first log reached this sea stack. She never seems to be afraid of it. Have you seen her at the adjoined tables with Dandelion?"

"Not yet." Beth replies as she slips off her shoes and tucks her legs so her toes touch the edge of the golden stone. Looking into its intense glow, she moves her feet under the sleeping animals until she feels the energy of the stone.

Watching her closely, Ann sees the stone become brilliantly translucent and fluid-like forms swirl within its shape. At that moment, both animals move away from the stone and lay down a few feet away. Ann shouts, "My god, Beth, what are you doing to that stone? It looks as if it came alive when your feet touched it."

Smiling at her, Beth says, "Put your toes on the stone. Don't be afraid. Let yourself feel the stone's energy. Let the energy talk to you. Know that whatever you receive is meant for you and only you. Each of us feels the energy differently. Though there is only one stone, it reacts to each of us as individuals. Always remember this, the golden stone here in the floor in the same in all of our homes. It and the touchstones in the cliff face on the north and south cliffs are the same for all of us and have never been anywhere else but where they are. These stones are the connection for Elizabeth Ann Anderson and Dana Marie Anderson no matter where we go or how we differ. These stones are the one consistent factor in our dimension."

Ann moves her feet on to the golden stone and smiles at Beth, saying, "It's warm. Is that what you feel?"

"Move them out a bit if it gets uncomfortable. That's why the animals love to sleep on top of it. Choose a time of day that is best for you to come and try to get here every day for at least a month, then whenever you can. Liz and I run to the cliffs in the morning and sit at the adjoined table afterwards until around noon. That seems to be the best time for us. Where you are sitting fits into the seating arrangement the three of us have at the adjoined tables."

"Good. I like to sit facing the forest with my back to the ocean. It seems to help me concentrate on the stone's energy."

"I'll tell the others where to watch for you and expect to see you there, if and when you do come through. I'm sure it will go smoothly once you get your routine established and are comfortable with the stone's energy. I'm certain our dimensions will open to yours and you'll be at the adjoined tables whenever you wish, even when we're not there."

Ann is silent as Beth talks to her, then, she whispers, "Beth, I'm seeing the inside of a cabin around me. Is it yours? There's a bentwood rocker over by a fireplace next to a brown leather sofa."

"Yes, Ann, we've come into my dimension. I'm home. Don't stand up. We're sitting under my dining table. See how the stone in my floor didn't change from the one in your sea stack. Good for you for noticing. Even Honey came with us. Hey, Dandelion, we're home." Instantly, the cat sits up and meows.

Ann exclaims, "Honey and Dandelion must have met each other before today. While I was building the last of the bridges, Honey laid on the golden stone often. I'll bet she came through to your dimension without my realizing it. Should I meditate every time I come to the stone?"

"It would probably be a good idea as it would help you get used to its energy. Also, the three of us are usually here at meal times, six, noon and six. Those are your best chances to meet the others at the adjoined tables."

Suddenly, Ann begins to cry and Beth reaches out to comfort her. When her hand touches Ann's shoulder, both Ann and Honey vanish and Dandelion lays down on top of the golden stone. Petting the purring cat, Beth says, "Well, Dandy, I guess that ends our visit with Ann and Honey for today."

Pulling her legs around, Beth crawls out from under the table and a voice she knows shouts, "Holy moly, Aunt Beth? What in the world are you doing under the table?"

Looking up, Beth sees her niece Nicole standing in front of the kitchen counter holding sacks of groceries in both arms. "Well, young lady, I could say the same to you. What in the world are you doing down at the beach at this time of day? Don't you have finals this week?"

Laughing, Nicole takes Beth's hands and helps her to her feet. When Beth's upright, Nicole wraps her in a bear hug and says, "Finals are over and I needed beach time. I've a week till grades are posted and I find out whether I passed or failed. Is it all right if I stay?"

"More than all right. Come on, let's get the rest of your stuff. Is there much?" Beth asks as she follows Nicole out to the open car door. Taking a sack Nicole hands her, Beth heads back inside. Setting the sack next to the others on the kitchen counter, she turns and sees Nicole is standing in the open doorway with a puzzled look on her face. "Aunt Beth, it looks as if you've got company."

Expecting the company to be Lucy Wong, Beth is surprised to see a black car slowly making its way down the drive to where the women are standing by the entry steps. "I don't have the slightest idea who this is, do you?"

"Yes, he's Mom's doctor from the sanitarium in Salem. What the hell can he want?"

Both women walk to the front of the entry deck and watch the man open his car door, step out and smile at them. When neither of them responds, the man stops at the front of his car. Then Nicole turns to Beth and says, "I don't like the looks of this son-of-a-bitch one bit, Aunt Beth. Should I get your shotgun, shoot him first and ask questions later?"

"Let him do the talking. After all, there are two of us and if he tries anything I'll just kick his balls to a bloody pulp. Is that a deal?"

Laughing, Nicole replies, "Right-O, Aunt B. Sounds like a plan. I forget what a tough broad you are."

"Yup, howdy, that's me. I'm one mean bitch." Beth laughs.

Hearing their patter, the man responds with a nervous chuckle and takes a step towards them. Before he can say a word, Nicole points at him. "Don't you take another step, Berry, just explain why you're here. My Aunt Beth is known for her kick punts to the groin."

The man stops, clears his throat, and says, "I'm here to talk to Beth. Her sister, Dee McGowan wants to see her. I wasn't expecting to find you here, Nicole. It's Beth that I wanted to speak to, not you."

"I have nothing to say to you either, Berry. I said it all when I testified against Dee at her trial for shooting to kill me. That's why she was committed to your sanitarium to be locked up for the next ten years. Don't you remember that?"

"Right, um, well, um, Beth, I wasn't sure you'd remember who I was. You're right, I'm Chet Berry, Dr. Berry, Dee's doctor at the sanitarium near Salem. I've written you twice this month asking you to come down to see your sister. She wants very much to see you and make amends. She saw Nicole last week and said it helped her so much as she was able to vent some of her anger. Later, she told me how pleased she was by your visit, Nicole. She thought you felt the same. Was it as good for you, Nicole?"

Raising her hand to stop her niece from answering, Beth says, "First off, Dee never wrote or phoned me. Nor have you, Berry. If you have, you obviously didn't check the address as the letters never got to me. It doesn't matter though as I'll never speak to my sister again."

Then Nicole walks over to stand in front of the man and answers the man's question. "No, Berry, the visit wasn't good for me. Dee was her usual hateful self. It took two of your men to pull her off of me. You had to have read that report. She was, and is, the bitch she has always been. I will not see her ever again. She punched and scratched my face and arms before the men rescued me from her. Why would you ever think I'd give a damn about her, after that? She has nine years left in her sentence and, as far as I am concerned, she can rot in hell."

"How can you say that, Nicole? Dee's your mother. How can you turn away from your mother?"

Without a word, Nicole moves away from him just as Lucy Wong's pickup truck turns off Shoreline Drive and stops behind Nicole's car. When Lucy jumps out, she greets Nicole with a hug and the two women whisper to each other for a few minutes. From where she stands, Beth hears just enough to know Nicole is explaining about the man now walking towards the younger women.

When Lucy sees him coming towards them, her face hardens dramatically as she shouts, "Stay where you are, Berry. Get back in your car and get the hell away from my friends and never come back here, ever. Don't say a thing, just drive like hell and get away from me and from my friends."

"Why it's Lucy Wong. Darling Lucy? How great it is to see you again. I didn't know you were up this way. What brings you out to these parts?" Ignoring Lucy's warning entirely, Chet Berry beams at the dark haired beauty standing next to Nicole as he walks towards them. Then, seeing the fierce look on both faces, Berry stops midway and turns back to Beth explaining, "Years ago, Lucy was my teaching assistant at Oregon State. Where did you end up, Lucy? Not in medicine, I see."

Lucy hisses at the man, "I changed directions once I broke away from your grasp and went into Oceanography and Biology. The air's much fresher out here and the field is more to my liking. In the ocean, there is only one deadly snake and there's a vaccine for its bite. You're bite would kill the snake. By the way, asshole, it's Dr. Lucy Wong."

The man looks stunned and backs to the rear of his car, "Oh come on, Lucy. I mean Dr. Wong? Won't you let bygones be bygones? What happened between us was years ago. We were young and foolish. When you vanished, I didn't know where you went. If I'd known you were nearby, I'd have come to find you before now. I'm here to ask Beth to visit her sister, Dee McGowan, Nicole's mother. She's one of my patients."

Turning to Nicole, he pleads, "Your mother would like to talk with you, too, Nicole. She wants to assure you of her love and to apologize for how she treated you when you told her you were lesbian and for how she rejected you so terribly last week. She said she'd written you an apology. When you didn't respond, I told her I'd carry her message to you and Beth. Here are her letters to you both."

Nicole's reaction is pure shock, then her face flushes bright pink and her eyes flash with anger as she shouts at the man. "How can I get through to you, asshole? Not for all the money in the world would I go to see that bitch again. Never. Tell Dee she's no longer my mother. Tell her that she is dead to both Nancy and me. She no longer has any daughters. Our only parent is Dr. Ed McGowan, our father. So, you go straight to hell and take those letters with you. I'll never forgive her for what she did to me and, most of all, I'll never forgive her for trying to kill Aunt Beth. Get in your car and get the hell out of here."

Beth claps her hands and roars with laughter, "Well said, darling Nicole. That goes twice for me, Berry-boy. Get the hell out of here and tell Dee what we said. Shove off, Berry, your car door is open. Get in it and get the hell out of here."

Looking totally dejected, Berry climbs back into his car and backs it onto Shoreline Drive. When the car disappears around the south curve, the three women share a group hug and cheer.

Then Nicole turns to Lucy and says, "Before the asshole stopped here, Aunt Beth and I were carrying my things inside. Any chance you can stay for dinner? I bought three great looking steaks just in case you could."

"Love to." Lucy exclaims.

NINE

June 10th—Eliza

ELIZA pushes her face up to the bathroom mirror, staring at new wrinkles on her forehead. Pulling the skin up towards the top of her head, she sighs, "Your age is showing, old girl. Time marches on so they say. It's only ten days since Marie's death and you look as if you've aged ten years. Hell, I feel as if it's been ten years. Life is so empty without her and the twins. I don't know what I'd have done without working daily in Mary Trimble's shop. Those hours are the only ones that give me a bit of relief from my pain."

Turning away from the mirror, she walks to her bed and slowly dresses in the clothes she'd laid out before her shower. Shifting and tugging each piece of clothing until satisfied with the fit, she finally goes out the door of her suite and crosses to Marie's. This door is wide open, there are no signs of anyone having lived in there. Nothing is out of place. Going through to the door of the dressing room, she stares at the empty rods and shelves.

Then she turns to the bank of cabinets covering the longest wall. Opening the doors, she starts pulling out the winter clothing stored there and places the items on the bed. Working methodically, she pops open the moving boxes she'd used the week before and packs each of them as full as she can. When the cabinets are empty and each box is full, Eliza carries them out to her car.

Returning to the room, she checks to make certain the closets and cabinets are empty. Once she is sure there is nothing more of Marie in the suite, Eliza closes the doors and goes back down to the fully loaded car. Starting the engine, Eliza wonders if Mary Trimble will be in at the shop when she gets there and looks forward to Mary's warm greeting.

Releasing the brake, she lets the car back slowly onto the drive and pushes the remote to again close the garage door. It's then that she sees the bottom half of a woman standing where her car had been parked. However, the closing door blocks the view to the woman's upper torso. Gasping, Eliza slams on the brakes and pushes the remote button to reopen the door.

Jumping out of the car, she rushes into the empty garage, shouting, "Marie? Are you in here? I know you were in your room today as I packed the last of your things. Do you have something to say to me? These are the last of your things and I'm taking them to that shop I've been volunteering at, the one that helps abused women and children. I work there every day as it helps me not miss you so much. I'll never forget you, my darling sister. I love you."

When she sees nothing and there is no response, Eliza turns to go back to her car but is shocked by a woman's shadowed form, backlit by the sun, standing in the middle of the open garage doorway. Rushing up to the ominous form, Eliza shouts, "Who are you? What do you want?"

"Eliza? It's me, Penny, your neighbor from next door. I'm so sorry if I frightened you. We've been wondering about how you are doing. So, I decided to come over and see you for myself. Is someone here with you? I didn't mean to interrupt your conversation."

Walking to the woman's side, Eliza laughs nervously, "My God, Penny, you scared the hell out of me. With the sun behind you I thought you were Marie. Don't worry about me, I'm fine. I'm taking the last of Marie's thing down to The Open Door Shoppe in Ocean Shores. By the way, if you're in the mood to shop and need something nice to wear, you should go to The Open Door Shop. Marie had wonderful taste in everything. The money goes to help abused women and children. Tell Al 'Hi' for me. When's the next game night? Call me if you want to set something up, okay? I'd love to host a gathering if no one else wants to do it."

Talking as she get into her car, Eliza starts the engine, gives a quick wave to Penny, the starts to leave. Seeing her neighbor still standing at the side of her driveway, Eliza opens the car window on that side and calls out, "Thanks for your concern, Penny. We'll get together soon. It's time I get back to seeing everyone again."

Turning onto Shoreline Drive, she catches sight of her neighbor's face in the rearview mirror and sees the grimace on the woman's face. "Oh dear, Marie, I think I stepped all over Penny's toes. Now she knows I'm crazy for sure. Damn, I really do need that white dog to be here all the time. Then I can talk to him and nobody will think I'm crazy."

A half hour later, Eliza parks in a space not far from entrance to The Open Door Shoppe. When she gets out and walks toward the front door, the large white dog appears to the right of the entry door. Frowning, she stops and stares at the animal. Then she laughs, saying, "My god, I'm being dogged by a ghost dog. How perfectly appropriate for someone who is slowly losing her hold on reality in leaps and bounds."

At this she laughs again, "Leaps and bounds? Really, Eliza, you've got to stop giggling at your own jokes or you'll be sitting in a padded cage bound by a white coat. Literally fit to be tied."

Walking towards the white dog, she waits beside it as a couple women come out the shop's door. When they pass the dog, she sees that they move away from him and mutter about dogs off leashes. Surprised but pleased that they see the animal, Eliza enters the shop with a smile on her face. Going to the clerk called Lisa, she says, "Hi Lisa, I've brought the last load of my sister's things. Could you help me bring them inside? I'll do the cataloging for the inventory. Will Mary be in today?"

"I'll be glad to help you. Mary was in, but stepped out to go to the bank. She'll be back by the time we've brought the boxes inside."

Leading the clerk to her car. Eliza glances down at the white dog and smiles. Within minutes, the two women have everything unloaded to the room at the back of the shop and Eliza starts to inventory the items, as Lisa returns to assist customers. By the time, the shop manager, Mary Trimble, returns from her errands, Eliza is finishing the last box and happily humming an old tune as she lists the items on the forms.

"Eliza, what a nice surprise to find you here. Lisa told me you brought the rest of Marie's things. I'm so glad. Most of what you brought last week has already sold. Her things are so lovely they nearly fly off the racks. I don't often tell customers where items come from. This time, I do whenever anyone asks about one of her items, I tell them Marie's story. Everyone says to thank you for donating her wonderful things to this great cause and I'll say it again, for all of us, thank you so much, Eliza. Thinking of us at your time of sorrow makes your generosity twice as wonderful."

As Mary speaks, tears suddenly flow down Eliza's cheeks and the store manager exclaims, "Oh my dear, I'm so sorry if I made you cry."

Putting her arms around Eliza's shoulders, Eliza shakes her head and says, "No, don't be sorry. It's just hit me that this load of her things are the last visual reminder of Marie and, in so many ways, are the proof that she lived and what a classy lady she was."

As Eliza talks, Mrs. Trimble pushes her gently into a chair next to the table and says, "Sit for a while, Eliza. You're just realizing how final Marie's death is, how final all deaths are. It often takes weeks for the people left behind to do the same. Your broken life will heal slowly and you'll find new ways to fill your days. You were numb from the shock of her death when you brought Marie's things a week ago. Now you've had time for it to soak in. On top of that, you've brought the physical proof of Marie's long existence. Most people don't take on this ordeal for months after a loved one dies.

"However, I believe your way is the best way. You've released her things for the good they can do. Now Marie can fly free and go on her journey. You have your memories and you have photographs. You don't need things to remind you of Marie or who she was. In your heart you know exactly what she meant to you and that's what matters most."

Picking up the forms listing Marie's things, Mary says, "I see you've not only listed each of the items but already have them priced for display. I'm very impressed, Eliza. I wonder if it's too soon to ask something I've been thinking about. Would you like to be scheduled to work here on a regular basis? Lisa returns to the U next week and we've been very busy."

"Yes, I'd love to do that. It's such a joyful place to come to. I love the feeling I get when I'm helping others." Eliza replies.

Late in the afternoon, Eliza says goodnight to Mary and Lisa and leaves the shop to get into her car. Seeing that the white dog is no longer sitting next to the shop's door, she tells herself, "Maybe a dog catcher took him off. I haven't thought of him the whole day."

Then, Eliza realizes that she is worrying about what she is certain is a ghost dog and she smiles all the way out of Ocean Shores. As she turns onto Shoreline Drive and starts to pick up speed, she sees the large dog, in the rearview mirror, running behind the car. Stopping the car on the shoulder of the road, she rolls the window down and shouts, "Hey Whitey, get in the car. I'm sure we're going to the same place."

In that second, the dog vanishes from the road and reappears on the back seat of her car. Surprised by how quickly the change was made, Eliza laughs out loud and says, "Well, howdy, my friend, I'm beginning to think there is much more to you than I ever imagined. Will you talk to me like Kip does to Liz? No? That's okay, just wag your tail if something pleases you."

As she drives, Eliza feels the dog watching her from the back seat until she turns down the driveway and pushes the remote to open the garage door. When the door rolls up in front of her, she sees the dog sitting next to the door into the house. Looking in the rearview mirror, she sees that the back seat of the car is empty.

Walking past the dog, she opens the door to go into the house and stops. Looking back at the dog, Eliza says, "Come in, Whitey. Go lay down on the golden stone under the dining table. Maybe you'll meet Kip and Dandelion."

To her surprise, the large white dog does as she said and curls around the glowing stone. Shaking her head, Eliza says, "Welcome, my friend. My house is your house. Either that or I'm just plain crazy."

From the dining table, a voice says, "Yes, that's always a possibility. However, I've always thought of you as the saner one of the three of us. What happened to make you so sure you're crazy?"

Seeing Liz sitting at the end of the adjoined tables, Eliza laughs. Then she sees that Kip is lying next to the white dog at the golden stone. Staring at the animals, Eliza says, "How you startled me, Liz. I thought that white dog had finally decided to speak to me. I'm glad to see it was you instead. Tell me, when you look down at Kip lying next to the golden stone, do you see a large white dog beside him?"

"Yes, I see a white dog. Is he yours? Kip seems to think he's okay." Liz says, "How long have you had him?"

"I'm so glad you see him. It seems no one else did until today. He came to me the night Marie and the twins were killed in that plane crash. He goes wherever I go. I just gave it a ride home from the shop where I took Marie's things. As the garage door opened, it was already waiting at the door into the house. I invited it inside tonight as it won't come in without an invitation. What does Kip say about the animal. Oh for heavens sakes, the dog's disappeared again. Kip's over the whole stone. Go figure…"

"Does this white dog talk to you as Kip does to me?"

"No and I wish it would. At first I was frightened by it and yelled at it in front of other people. They thought I was yelling at them as they couldn't see the white dog even though it was right in front of them. Even though it came after Marie's death, I don't get a sense of why it's here. At least I'm no longer afraid of it anymore. This morning I actually missed it when I didn't see it on the deck. Have you ever heard of such things happening?"

"If it will ease your mind, there's a beautiful white dog lying on your brown leather sofa. Did you give it permission to do that?" Liz asks Eliza.

Turning, Eliza sees the white dog on the sofa and goes over to it. Putting her hand on top of its head, she is surprised when the animal doesn't disappear. Instead, he looks up at her with his golden eyes as she smooths its fur. Running her hand down the length its body, she feels its muscles flex as her fingers smooth its silky coat and as she scratches between its ears, the animal heaves a big sigh.

Liz laughs, "I heard that sigh all the way over here. Your white dog sighed just like Kip does. Whenever I give his ears a good scratching, he heaves a big sigh and often smiles with a wrinkled nose grin. Maybe your dog will talk to you in the future. I love that I can ask Kip things about people we meet and if there are things I should know."

"It'd certainly be nice to know why he came here. I keep calling him Whitey though I doubt that is his name. I feel he's waiting for something to happen so he can save me. Does that sound stupid?"

"Not at all. He is a beautiful dog and I'm sure you'll enjoy having him with you now that you're alone. The house was very empty before Kip came to me."

Looking over at the white dog on the white leather sofa, Eliza smiles, "Yes, I'll admit it is very nice to see him sleeping there and not just trying to get my attention. Tonight, it just seemed right that I ask him to come in the house."

TEN

June 15ᵗʰ—Liz

LIZ runs beside Kip as they head towards the north cliffs. Her thoughts are on what Beth told her about Ann Anderson's dimension. Since the first time Kip took her into the crystal room, they have returned to the amazing cave every day. Today she's determined to enter Ann Anderson's dimension and as they crosses the granite slab, Liz tells Kip, "Okay, let's concentrate on going in to Ann Anderson's dimension. Are you ready?"

As I'll ever be.

His words lighten her mood and she slaps the touchstone and gleefully shouts, "I declare this run good and done."

Instantly, the dimension turns into one she's never seen before. As she stands in front of the touchstone, it begins to move out of the cliff face with a scraping noise. Backing away, she sees it grow over twelve feet long, tip downwards and slide off the edge of the granite. When it hits the beach below, the tip jams between the rocks and gravel covering the tide flats.

Almost certain that she's in Ann Anderson's dimension, Liz calmly watches as steps appear in the elongated touchstone. When the steps are complete, she moves towards it to climb down. However, Kip rushes past her, races down the long stone and onto the rocky tide flats to greet a large golden dog running to meet him. The dogs bark joyously as they greet each other, then race onto shore and disappear up a trail into a forested hillside.

Surprised by Kip's actions, Liz shouts, "Kip, stay. Kip, come." Her shout turns the dogs and they race back to the stone stairs below the granite slab. Barking frantically until Liz climbs down to the rocky tide flats and follows them. Weaving around large rocks and boulders across a hundred feet of tide flats, she climbs the steep path up to the high shoreline.

Once on the trail, she turns to follow the dogs into the woods covering the hillside, when she hears a shout from the clifftops. Looking up, she sees a woman on the cliff tops waving at her. "Hey, come up here. If that's Kip with Honey you must be Liz. Come up here. We'll go to my house from here. The tide's just going out, so we have hours before you have to get back to the touchstone. How's everything in your dimension? It's been stormy here the past few days. Today's sunshine is a wonderful surprise."

Laughing with the woman's enthusiasm, Liz hurries up the trail to where this new Elizabeth Ann Anderson waits. When she gets to where she can see the stone structures Beth had described, Liz exclaims, "Wow, Ann, what a wonderful area you've created up here. Beth was right when she said I would love it."

"Wow, yourself, Liz. Beth has told me so much about you that I feel I already know you. Love your cropped hair. I just may have mine cut that short."

"Thanks. I keep it short as I hate hair flying in my face. It's always windy on my beach. As you said, this joyful beast next to me is Kip and that beauty must be Honey. Kip told me they've known each other many lifetimes."

Suddenly, the two dogs go over to both woman, sniff them, look from one woman to the other and finally sit beside their own mistress. The women laugh at the animals' confusion and that is enough to send the dogs racing down the trail and into the woods. Only their joyous barking tells the women where they are.

"I'm so relieved that I've finally gotten here." Liz exclaims as she gives Ann a hug, "Beth said if I thought of you from the time I left home until I slapped my touchstone, I'd get here. However, I tried that every morning this week and I kept going to the crystal cave. I don't know what I did differently this morning, but here I am."

Seeing Ann's smile, Liz says, "I'm sure Beth told you that I found a cave with a large crystal room. It's very beautiful and I love being in there. However, I am so happy to finally meet you and am looking forward to seeing your wonderful place. Beth has told me about everything here, but I can't wait to see it for myself."

"It's great to meet you, Liz. Aren't we Elizabeth Ann's amazing? When I first met Beth, I had a hard time accepting who or what she was. Now I expect her to come here every day. Yesterday was the fifth time she's come through to me, but she didn't come today. No matter how much she's told me about you, I need a hug to be sure I'm not dreaming and that you're really here with me."

"Me too, Ann. Yup, you're real." Liz laughs and steps back to study this new Parallel Life. Then, hearing the dogs barking somewhere in the woods, she says, "We don't have to worry about them. Kip is truly awesome. He always knows the right thing to do."

"I know what you mean, My Honey knows what's going to happen before it happens. After she met Beth, Honey was terribly confused by our sameness. Now she's the first to greet her and Dandy when they come here. Still, it was cute to see how puzzled those two were about us, wasn't it? They finally figured out who was who by our smell. It's great that Honey has another dog to run through the woods and be a real dog for a change."

"Yes, I'm sure Kip loves it as well. Though, I'm not too certain they can ever be real dogs. Kip is so much more. Oh, oh... here they come again, barking for us to follow them. Do you think we'd better go?"

"Yes or they won't stop barking till we do." Ann laughs. Then, she points south to the basalt outcropping where a framework shows and says, "First, I want to point out where Dad's cabin sat before it was swept out to sea. That tsunami took the entire beach and most of the adjoining land. My family was very fortunate that the storm warnings sounded too terrible so we stayed home. No one expected the earthquakes and tidal waves to hit at the same time that storm did. They did and it was terrible.

"Hundreds of people were swept away or killed by falling debris. It took the cabin and broke Dad's heart. He couldn't talk about it for over a year. I was ten when the cabin was swept away. Four years later a drunk ran through a stop sign and took all of them, Dad, Mom and Dana, away from me."

As she tells her story, Ann's eyes fill with tears as she stares at the basalt outcropping to the south. "Everything's gone that was here. Only the floor of Dad's cabin is left. Did Beth tell you about the bridges I built over the gaps between those basalt stacks? The day I first showed her what I'd done, the two of us sat at the golden stone and, after a few minutes, I saw her cabin around us. We were under her table."

Liz studies the barren mile to the south and realizes what Ann must have felt when her family died. "To lose your family after losing the cabin must have been horrible for you. At least Beth, Eliza and I have had Dad's cabin all our lives. Since the golden agate is still there, I'm surprised you haven't come through our adjoined tables. We meet almost daily to update on what's happening in our lives."

"I know that. However, now that the bridge is done, I've started building a sturdy shelter over the end with the golden stone. I hope to do most of it myself, though I'll have the roof done by contractor I know. I'll only cover the western third of the floor. The rest I'm leaving open for landings with seating areas under wide overhangs. I used baling wire to hold the drift logs to the basalt stacks for the bridges and it's held tight through the storm that hit the beach the first of the week."

"It looks as if you've got a good start on the cabin. Could we walk down and see it before we go up to your place?"

"Not today. There's so much I want you to see up at the house. Let's wait until I come through to the adjoined tables. Then you can take all the time you like to look over what I did. Beth told me that you found the plans for Dad's cabin at Portland's Main Library. So, I called that same day and one of the clerks offered to copy a set for me. I picked them up the next day after work."

"How nice of her. Don't you love seeing how much thought he gave to planning it? Just looking at them brings Dad back to me. He was such a dear man. I have them hung over the fireplace and look at them every day."

"Beth said that you had done that. I like that idea, so I'm going to hang mine in my cabin near the freestanding stove I'll put in there. Though it's only a third of the original cabin's size, it's out over the beach. I know the authorities will make certain that I've been ecologically astute in what I do out there. I'm installing a propane stove and lights, a two piece bath with a Swedish composting toilet and sink and a queen sized bed so Honey and I can have comfortable sleepovers whenever we want."

"Oh, Ann, that sounds wonderful. Has Beth told you how the touchstones have told her that are to meet in the crystal room on the Summer Solstice? Good. Evidently if we get there before sunrise and are all there, we will stay together so all time. Beth told me the opening in the cave's ceiling exits onto the top of your cliffs. If so, that should make it easy for you to get there no matter what the weather. Evidently this Summer Solstice is very important for the Parallel Lives of Elizabeth Ann. Please, don't miss it."

Then Ann points up the trail where the two dogs are sitting in the middle of the trail into the woods. "I think we're getting eyed. We'd better get over to those dogs or they are going to come down and drag us up there."

Following Ann to where the dogs wait, Liz is pleased at how at ease Ann is with her and decides that her knowing Beth the past week has readied her to meet other Parallel Lives. "I'm certain once you're comfortable with the energy from the golden stone, you'll come through to the adjoined tables whenever you want, Ann. After all, you are an Elizabeth Ann Anderson. Beth told us that you like to sit facing the room with your back to the ocean. That's good, as I always sit facing the ocean and Beth and Eliza sit at either end of the table."

When they come to the high point of the trail, Liz stops to take a long look at the vista below and says. "I'll tell you one thing, Ann, you're in much better shape than I am. I'm not used to climbing steep hills so fast. Whew. Give me a minute to catch my breath. Is your house much further?"

Ann laughs. "Sorry, I forget that I do this four or five times a day. My house is just past that group of bushes. Take your time. I'll go ahead as I'm too excited about showing off my home to stand still. Come when you're ready and I'll show you all the stuff darling Aunt Margret stored. It's everything from my family's home and, after I graduated from the University, she took me to the storage unit and handed me the key. What an amazing gift she gave me.

"Those boxes held so many memories and more. She'd even wrapped an ashtray filled with my folks' cigarette butts and I've saved it exactly as I found it. Whenever I feel blue, I unwrap it, breathe deeply and, for a few seconds, Mom and Dad are with me again. I'm so lucky. Though my family is gone, I have so many things that keep them close to me and I give you permission to snoop through the house and enjoy yourself."

When she gets to Ann's house, there is such a familiarity about it that Liz stops to study the building. Then she realizes that even though it sits on a massive stone outcropping near the top of a hill, it is built almost exactly as her own house. As she steps onto the entry deck to the front door, she sees the ocean vista to the west and exclaim, "Ann, your view is spectacular. I can see for miles and miles. I'm so impressed. How wonderful to be so high and know all the land you see is yours."

Turning back to the glass slider doors on the front of Ann's home she instantly realizes why it seemed she'd been to the house before. "Ann, do you realize that you've built your own version of Dad's cabin, here on the hill. How wonderful to be up so high. I've never thought of living anywhere but on the beach. However, this view is stunning."

Feeling Kip nudge her leg, Liz looks at him and asks, "Would you like living in the trees instead of on the beach?"

Both are good.

Just then, Ann calls from the open slider doorway, "Liz, come inside and close the door after you. That wind really whistles through the house up this high."

Though reluctant to leave the wonderful view, Liz does as asked and finds Ann in her kitchen. Again Liz realizes Ann's shaped her house on her memory of her Dad's cabin. Even the hardwood floors gleam a dark ebony just as the polished cement floor in her own home does. Here and there, her mother's Turkish rugs add their colorful glory to Ann's home, just as they do in her own home.

Dazzled by the many items on display that are the same as those in her home, Liz moves slowly through the open room trying to take it all in. One by one, she recognizes items she remembers but no longer has and is thrilled to see them again. Touching each, Liz remembers the times she'd used or played with them when she was a child.

"Memories are everywhere I look." Liz says as she helps Ann bring their lunch plates to the dining table. Pointing to a painting over the fireplace, "That hung in our living room in Portland, right over our sofa. Mom's father, Carl Aaron Bloom, painted it. Now it hangs over my bed. That handmade doll sitting on the wicker chest is exactly like mine that sits on my bentwood rocker next to my bed. I named her Candice. Mom made her for Christmas the year I was six."

"The same for me, to everything you say, Liz. Dana and I got our dolls that year, too. The doll is wonderful to have, isn't it? Whenever I hold it, I feel the love Mom poured into making it for me. Dana says she feels the same way. Beth said she'd had a doll like it, but it was lost when the family had to evacuate the cabin when those storms hit."

Liz says. "Seeing all these things is like rediscovering my past. Beth was right to insist I visit your dimension. However, don't let me get too comfortable and forget about the time. I don't know what would happen if I have to stay overnight."

"Don't worry, I've set the timer. We've got several hours. Come and eat, then I'll give you a tour of the house and you can snoop through everything."

The hours pass quickly as the women share the same memories of items in Ann's home. When the timer sounds, the sun has moved towards the west and the wind is sending waves past the sea-stacks near the western end of the cliffs. Both women know Liz must get back to the touchstone and they call the dogs to follow as they head down the trail. Kip and Honey race ahead and wait for them at the edge of the shoreline.

Hugging Ann, Liz says, "Remember to come to the crystal room on the Summer Solstice. Keep sitting at your golden stone and we'll spend time together at the tables. Bring Honey so she can play with Kip on the beach. Okay?"

Seeing Ann's tearful nod, Liz gives her a kiss on the cheek, rubs Honey's head, and says, "Come on, Kip, it's time to go home."

When she and Kip stand in front of the golden stone on the cliff face, Liz waves at Ann and Honey on the shoreline and yells, "See you later, alligator."

Ann waves both hands high over her hand and cheers, "After while crocodile." Then Liz slaps the touchstone and shouts, "I declare this run good and done."

ELEVEN

June 15ᵗʰ—Beth

BETH is sitting at the adjoined tables when Liz comes through to her. "Please stay with me a while, Liz. I must talk to you. This morning's session at the touchstone was frightening. That darned stone locked onto me the way it did to you when Kip went through his changes. It held me for over an hour. All that while, strong surges of energy flowed through me. It was exhausting and frightening. I've never felt like that before and I don't want to feel like that again. There is no question these messages can be ignored, so listen carefully."

For the next several minutes, Beth relates the information from the touchstone to Liz. "Even though it told me before that we should be in the crystal room by sunrise on the Summer Solstice. This time the message insisted that whoever didn't meet in the crystal room before sun rise would be lost to the others forever. Please, Liz, if you see Eliza, tell her to go to the crystal room directly or to come here and go with us. She must not go into another dimension ever again, ever."

Liz nods, "I wish there were some way to call her or leave a note for her at the tables. She's so blasé about going to other dimensions. She considers doing it one of the great adventures of being a Parallel Life of mine. The only dimensions she can go into are here at the adjoined tables or to the crystal room and, if she doesn't come with us, we'll lose our connection with her."

Beth says, "I know it sounds the same as I told you the other day, Liz, but this time the intensity was very extreme. By the time the stone released me, I was exhausted and shaking. On the Solstice meet me here by four AM. We'll run together to the touchstone and go into the crystal room at the same time. If we do that, we'll be protected for all time. The stone said that once we do this we'll be able to travel safely between dimensions and our connections to each other will stay strong."

When Beth stops talking, Liz sees her hands shake and replies, "I was in Ann's dimension this morning and told her about meeting us on the Summer Solstice in the crystal room. She assured me she'll be there very early. She say's to tell you that she's gotten a good start on her cabin over the golden stone in the cement floor of her Dad's old cabin. She's doing much of the framing but has hired a contractor to put up the shell and roof it."

"Well, isn't that wonderful. I'm so pleased for her. I'm surprised she's working so hard to get it done before she comes through to us." Beth says, "It's great that you went there today as I didn't go anywhere except back here after that stone let go of me. I'm not worried about Ann, she's very reliable and I'm sure she'll be in the crystal room as soon as we are. However, Eliza is another matter. She's gotten on an odd schedule since Marie died and seems to have disappeared. I'm afraid she's gone a bit over the edge."

"Not really, Beth. I saw her the other day and she was fine. She's been volunteering at a secondhand shop in Ocean Shores. The place where she took Maries things. The shop uses the funds to operate safe houses for abused women and children. Also, she's not alone anymore. A white dog came to her after Marie died. Kip told me he knows the animal from other lifetimes. Eliza said he doesn't talk to her as Kip does to me. Just stares at her with sad golden eyes. Connect with her later in the afternoon. I met her here around five thirty, as she volunteers at the shop until four or so. If I see her, I'll tell her everything you said. Right now I've got to get going, See you tomorrow morning for sure."

Before Beth can answer, both Liz and Kip vanish. At the same moment, Beth's front doorbell rings. Thinking Lucy has dropped by, she goes to the door and opens it without looking through the peephole. However, instead of Lucy, a man stands with his back to the door, staring down the south beach.

"Berry? What the hell brings you back here?" Beth shouts at the man's back.

Whirling around, the man exclaims, "Beth! Beth! Thank god you're all right."

"Why shouldn't I be all right? What's going on, Berry?"

"I tried to get you by phone and when you didn't answer I was worried she'd already gotten here. I left messages for you to call me, but you didn't. Why didn't you return my calls?"

"Damn it, Berry, you still have that wrong number. I'll say it again, I've not received any messages from you, ever. Not one." Then Beth stops and frowns. "Damn you, Berry, are you saying that Dee escaped from your facility in Salem? How long ago was that?"

"Forty-eight hours. We've searched everywhere in the sanitarium and anywhere else she could have gone in the community. The front gate security tapes show her driving away in one of the employee's cars. That was two days ago. We don't know how she got out of her ward and none of the vehicles have been reported missing. We don't know whose she was using. So far there's no sign of her. My god, Beth, I'm sick about it. You were right. Dee is a manipulator. She gets others to do what she wants them to do. When we bring her back, she will be locked up in her room with bars on the windows at all times, every second."

Frowning at the doctor, Beth steps back and shouts, "What do you mean, will be? The judge sentenced her to be locked in a secured room for nine years. Berry, you stupid asshole, you let her out to roam free? How did she get out? What did she do? Fuck you? Give you blow jobs?"

When the man turns crimson, she shakes her head and hisses at him, totally disgusted. "Get in here and tell me the whole story. You talk as I fix us lunch. Then, you go back out there and find Dee. When was the last time you called your office? They may have found her by now."

"For some reason, my cell phone doesn't work out here."

"None of them do. The closest cell tower is over the hills near Hoquiam. Use the landline phone on the kitchen counter." Beth points the direction to him as she shuts and locks the front door.

Making his calls, Berry asks questions and Beth listens to what is said. When he hangs up, he looks over at her with dismay. "Most of Dee's clothing is missing as well as two pillow cases from her room. The police think she may have headed south towards the Mexican border. Does she know anyone outside of the U.S? Someone in another country? Someone who'd put her up and not call the authorities? Is there a cabin or house she could go to and not be found? Do you think she might come here to stay with you?"

"You have got to be kidding, Berry. Do I have to say it again? Dee shot to kill me only a year ago. Almost did. That's why she was sentenced to a secured room in your sanitarium. Call her ex-husband. Tell him about this and ask him for information. I can't believe you haven't done it already. If she's not found soon, buster, you are in deep doo-doo. Personally, I hope they pull your license. What a stupid ass you've been."

"I love Dee so much. I was sure she loved me. I want to spend the rest of my life with her. I even left my wife and asked for a divorce so I could marry Dee. I wanted to keep her safe while she serves her sentence. Oh, dear God, what have I done?"

After a long pause, Berry says, "You're right, Beth, I'm dead in my field. No institution would take me again. I've gotten too involved with a patient. But what could I do? Dee was so wonderful, so loving and lovely. Oh dear God, what have I done? How could I have trusted her so much? Why was I so stupid?"

"Hell, Berry, you aren't the only sucker. Dee is the queen of manipulation. She was first institutionalized at eighteen. That's when she met and married her husband, Dr. Ed McGowan and it took him twenty years to realize that Dee has no conscience. In fact, at her trial last year, he told the courts that she becomes toxic to anyone who is in contact with her. You heard him say all that in court during her trial and yet you still fell for her charms. Damn, you are a fool."

"I loved her, Beth. I still do." Berry sobs into his hands. "What are you going to do? Can someone come and be with you until she's found."

"Don't worry about me, Berry. I bought a pistol after she shot me last year and have a permit to carry it on my body. I've used it many times target practicing on cans that wash up on the beach. It's here in this kitchen cabinet and I'm going to strap in over my shoulder right now. I'll keep it on me until she's caught. Dee's the one in danger if she comes here. I'll happily blast her to kingdom come as soon as I see her. So if you want to help her, go find her and take her back to Salem. Right now, I'm calling Nicole."

When her niece answers, Beth tells her, "Nicole, I'm calling to tell you that your mother escaped two days ago. Berry came here looking for her a few minutes ago. Evidently, she was not held in the secured room you saw her in and the one the court ordered her into. She has a forty-eight hour head start with two pillowcases filled with most of her things. Call your Dad and Nancy and warn them to take care. If they see her, they should call the police. In forty-eight hours, Dee could talk the devil into giving her a ride out of hell. You stay alert. Dee won't go to Seattle as there are too many people that know her.

"No, don't go to your apartment. Stay with friends. Don't be alone at any time. I understand you're busy. Stay that way and keep people around you at all times. After you talk to your father and Nancy, call me back. I'm going to be locked in my house until she's caught. No, Lucy isn't here right now. She went into town a bit ago. You're right, I'll call her now. I should have thought of that. Love you, kiddo, keep safe. We'll talk later."

When Beth finishes with her call, Berry takes the phone and calls his assistant at the sanitarium. When he is finishes, he turns to her with tear filled eyes and she asks, "What now?"

"One of the night nurses went missing before we knew Dee was gone. They've found the nurse's body under the trash bin behind the main building. She's been strangled. The car Dee was driving, in the security tape, belonged to this nurse. Now the State Police are fully involved and APBs are out on both Dee and the car. My assistant says her photograph is all over national news, both television and radio."

"What's the make and model of the car? I'd like that information for my local Sheriff and to alert Lucy Wong. I'm going to have her come here and stay with me tonight. Or better yet, I'll stay up there with her. If Dee left the hospital when you think she did, she could be walking down my driveway right now."

As soon as the words are out of her mouth, Beth runs to her bathroom to look out the window opening to the driveway. When Liz sees nothing unusual, she returns to the kitchen to find Chet Berry talking on the phone. Seeing her, Berry makes motions with his pen as if writing. Beth opens a drawer along the counter, takes out a note pad and hands it to him. Into the phone, Berry asks for the information to be repeated and, this time, writes down what he hears.

When he ends the call, he hands the paper to Beth. "The car Dee drove off in is a blue Toyota. This is the license number."

Beth frowns, "Dee might not realize anyone is on to her yet since the news just got out to the media. Her two day head start could put her anywhere. Right now, I'm calling Lucy. After that, you call Ed McGowan and explain everything. Tell him I'm fine and I've got my pistol on me. He should keep on alert as Dee could go after him."

When Beth connects with Lucy, she explains what happened and gives her the license number. Then she warns, "She's an attractive woman and looks normal. Don't be fooled and don't pick up any hitchhikers, no matter how pitiful they may look. Dee is a quick change artist. Remember that. Yes, I'm in my house. Chet Berry is here but he wants to leave in a short while. Honk when you get here and knock as usual. I've strapped on my pistol. Yes, I'll stay inside and be very careful. You too. Now? I'm making a strong pot of coffee and turning on the TV. The authorities have alerts out about her and someone may have seen her by now. Will you stay with me tonight? Thanks. See you later. OK, I will."

When both Beth and Dr. Berry have finished their calls, they sit at the dining table, sip coffee and stare at the small TV on the counter. Suddenly, Berry jumps to his feet and turns towards the front door. "Did you hear that? Is the door locked? I thought I heard a car."

"Don't just sit there, you damned fool, go check." Beth snaps at him, then races to the door herself. Berry kneels at the door with his ear pressed to the wood. "I hear something on the other side,' he whispers to Beth. As soon as he says the words, there is a loud rapping on the front door and both jump away from it, staring wide eyed at each other. Neither making a move.

Finally a deep voice hollers, "Beth? Hello? Beth? It's Tom Ames. Beth? Are you okay? My brother, George, called and told me he heard on the radio your sister escaped and might be heading this way. Beth, are you in there?"

Beth sighs with relief then shouts back, "I'm here, Tom, I'm alright. The lock seems to be stuck. Give me a moment to jimmy it a bit." As she talks to the man outside, she points at the table and pushes Dr. Berry towards it. Once he is seated, she unlocks and opens the door.

The worried look on her friend's face makes her smile, "Hi Tom. Thanks for coming to check on me. Dee's doctor is here as he thought she might have come this way. Have you two met?"

Beth's nerves cause her to over explain each man to the other, "Tom Ames and his brother, George, are two of the miracle workers who saved my cabin after the horrid storm last year. Dr. Berry is the head doctor at Oregon State's security sanitarium where Dee was sent for shooting me. Did you see anyone along the road in a bright blue Toyota sedan?"

Tom smiles at the other man as they shake hands, then tells her, "Now that you ask, I didn't see a single vehicle after I left Ocean Shores. Strange, huh?"

Leaving the two men, Beth rushes into the kitchen and refills the coffeemaker. "How about a fresh cup of coffee, Tom? If nothing else, it may help us settle down."

"No more for me." Dr. Berry says as he walks to the front door. "In fact, now that Tom's with you, I'm going back to my office. It's a five hour drive and I really should be there. I just wanted to catch Dee before the authorities and get her to turn herself in. If you see or hear anything about Dee, let me know." Without another word, he opens the door and goes out to the front of the house.

Following him out the door, Beth and Tom stop on the entry steps and watch Berry's car speed south on Shoreline Drive. At that time, Tom asks, "Do you always leave your truck parked out here with the garbage cans in the back?"

Beth frowns, "Oh damn, I took the garbage to the transfer station earlier this morning. I'll get the keys and open the garage. Will you get the cans out when I get it inside?"

When she runs back inside the house, Beth grabs the keys off the hook by the door and goes out to open the garage door. As the wide door rolls up to the ceiling of the garage, she realizes how vulnerable she is at that moment even though Tom now stands in front of the open door with a garbage can in each hand.

"Hang those on those large brass hooks on the back wall while I pull the truck inside."

"Glad to help," Tom chuckles as he takes the cans over to the back wall of the garage and hangs the cans on their brass hooks. Once she's behind the steering wheel, Beth releases the truck's parking brake and lets the pickup roll into the garage.

When the truck's parked, she gets out and Tom says, "I think right now you're glad I talked you into putting a door on the garage, am I right?"

Beth laughs, "I'll say I am. That remote door opener is the handiest thing."

As the two talk, they walk out to the driveway and become so involved in the details of their past projects that they don't notice a vehicle come down Shoreline Drive and turn down the driveway. Only when it stops a few feet behind them and its horn blasts do they jump around in fright. Then an angry voice shouts at them and Beth's pistol is no longer in its holster, it's in her hand.

"Hey, you two idiots, what the hell are you doing standing out here? You should be in the house. At the very least, you should have reacted when my truck came down the road. What was so damn important that you forgot Dee is out to kill Beth? Are you dumb or just plain stupid?"

Shaking from the fright, Beth and Tom slowly stand up from the low crouch they'd dropped into when the horn blasted, truly ready for anything. Seeing it is Lucy, Beth slips the pistol back into the holster before she shouts, "You rat faced clam-digger, I told you to honk when you got here. Why didn't you do it from the road? I almost shot you. I can't believe we didn't hear that tank of yours coming around the curve and down my driveway."

"Probably because you know its sound so well that it didn't red-flag you as a danger. You two must remember, Dee stole one car, killed a woman to get it, and probably won't stop at anything to get another shot at her sister. You must be more careful, Beth."

As Lucy finishes scolding Beth, she points a finger at Tom, "And you, big boy, you should know better. The wicked witch of the south is on the loose, what don't you understand about that? We have to keep Beth safe. Who the hell are you anyway?"

"What? You two don't know each other?" Beth exclaims, "Lucy Wong, this is Tom Ames. Tom this is Lucy Wong. Lucy is doing the survey for the Fish and Wildlife on the Maxine Oakley Beach Preserve for the State. Lucy, Tom is the miracle worker who braced up my cabin after the storm and built the dunes north of here which just passed your bosses' inspection. He did say the dunes looked really great, didn't he?"

"Yes, he did. Hi Tom, I'm very glad to meet you. As Beth said, you did a great job with those dunes." Lucy laughs as she shakes Tom's hand. "I'm here for that coffee, Beth, and I could even force down one or two of your day old brownies if you have any left. I'm starving."

As the three turn to go into the garage, a police car, sirens blaring and lights flashing, comes streaking up Shoreline Drive, slows and turns down Beth's driveway. Standing where they stopped at the back of Beth's pickup, the three watch the patrol car come to a stop next to Lucy's truck.

Instantly, the deputy jumps out and demands, "Which one of you is Beth Anderson?" Seeing Beth's hand raise, he continues, "I'm Deputy Brown. I'm to watch this end of the beach until they find your sister. They found the Toyota she stole in Longview. Two other cars have been reported missing in Elma. One was found abandoned in Aberdeen. So far there's no sign of your sister and we don't know if she stole either of the cars. But we strongly assume one of them was her doing. Who owns the trailer up the road??"

When Lucy waves her hand, the deputy talks directly to her, "Would it be possible for me to use it until McGowan is caught? It may be a couple days. I'll be able to see the length of the beach from there. Is there a key? Also is the space behind the trailer big enough to park the patrol car?"

"Yes to all that." Lucy tells him as she unclips the house key from her key ring and hands it to him. "Pull in at the back end of the trailer. The backdoor is there and halfway to the front. There's food in the fridge and cupboards. Make yourself at home. I'll be staying here with Beth until her sister is caught."

"Good idea." The deputy replies as he takes the key. At that moment, the patrol car's radio blares out a message and he hurries back to the vehicle to listen. Lucy turns to Beth and motions for her to get inside the house and close the garage door. "I'll tell you what the deputy has to report."

For a moment, Beth feels as if she's being sent to her room for being naughty, then she realizes Lucy just wants her safe so she goes into the garage and closes the door behind her. When she is inside the house, she checks the locks at the entry and the slider door to the beach deck. After that, she stands looking out at the north cliffs. It's then that she sees something moving near the granite slab.

Lifting the binoculars off their hook by the slider door, Beth steps outside to look through them. As she focuses the glasses, it seems a couple of strange people are making moves on each other. When the glasses are adjusted, Beth sees that the two are women. One is running out from Shoreline Drive and the other is stepping off the granite slab. Then, both move towards each other. When the women come close together, the runner catches the other into an embrace and for several seconds the two hold each other. Then the two seem to be doing an odd type of dance as they rock back and forth moving in jerky steps until they come against the granite slab.

At that moment, Beth understands what she sees and rushes out the slider door, screaming, "Dee's at the cliffs. Lucy and Tom. Tell the deputy Dee's at the cliffs."

As her friends run down the deck to her, Beth leaves the field glasses on the deck railing, jumps onto the sand below and races up the beach screaming at the women near the cliffs.

Shouting after her, Lucy screams, "Where the hell are you going? Beth?"

"What's happening?" Tom shouts as he picks up the field glasses and adjusts them to see the action at the cliffs.

Over her shoulder, Beth screams, "Dee's at the cliffs. Tell the Deputy to come. Come with me. Help me catch her."

Without another word, Beth runs with a purpose she's never known before. She recognizes the woman wrestling with Dee and she screams, "Run, Eliza, run." Over and over, the name leaves her mouth as she knows Eliza came into the wrong dimension and stayed too long. Now she's caught at the cliffs by a mad woman who wants to kill her, thinking she is Beth. This is the tragedy the touchstones saw. This is what they why they were warned.

Even though she is running faster than she ever has, Beth knows she is too late to help Eliza. They'll catch Dee, but they will not be able to help Eliza. Suddenly all action at the north cliffs seems to stop. Then, Beth sees Eliza fall to the sand. Dee lifts her head off the sand just as Beth screams Eliza's name and Dee knows she's killed the wrong Elizabeth Ann. Then, Dee shouts obscenities at Beth and plunges the knife into her own chest, seconds before the Deputy or Beth can grab it from her.

When they reach where Dee McGowan lies on the hard packed sand, the only sign that Eliza was ever there is one lone tress of white hair. As Beth lunges for it, the lone strand vanishes into the sand and Beth trips over Dee's body, splayed across the hard packed sand.

Smacking against the granite slab, Beth leans against the edge of the granite slab and rubs her bruised hands as she stares at where Eliza vanished. After checking to see if Beth is alright, the Deputy kneels beside Dee's body and feels for a pulse. Then he looks up at Beth, shakes his head and gently rolls the body onto its back.

At this time, both Tom and Lucy reach Beth and watch as the Deputy puts on rubber gloves, pulls the long knife from Dee's chest and drops it into a plastic evidence bag. Without comment, the Deputy turns away from them and carries the bag with the knife back to Shoreline Drive and his patrol car. Halfway there, the man turns back and shouts, "Don't touch anything on that body and stay there until I get back. I'm going to radio for assistance."

Lucy snorts, "As if any of us would."

Tom looks at Beth and says, "She's gone, Beth. Your sister Dee is gone. You'll never have to fear her again."

Nodding, Beth turns away from her friends, climbs onto the granite slab and crosses to the glowing stone in the cliff face. Leaning her forehead onto the golden agate, Beth whispers her last goodbye to Eliza. Then, standing tall, she slaps the translucent stone and shouts, "I declare this run good and done."

TWELVE

June 15ᵗʰ—Eliza's Last Morning

ELIZA is amazed at how fast her life has changed since Marie's death. Today is the first time she admits to herself that, though she misses her sister and wishes she were still alive, she enjoys the solitude of living alone again. She especially likes the time she spends working at The Open Door Shoppe with Mary Trimble and the other women there. For the last week, she hasn't sat once at the adjoined tables until she sits to eat her dinner in the evening.

This afternoon, she finds both Liz and Beth at the adjoined tables. When they see her come through to them, they both greet her rousingly and Liz shouts, "Beth and I were hoping you'd show up while we were here today. Beth has been receiving very intense warnings from the touchstone about what we're to do and not do on next week's Summer Solstice. You must stay and listen to her so she can tell you. It's very important."

Relieved to see Eliza's puzzled look, Beth says, "I can see you don't remember the touchstone's instructions I told you about a couple weeks ago. They were very specific about not going into unknown dimensions and to slap the touchstone immediately. The day we talked, you said you weren't going to live in fear as you thought we wouldn't be shown things if they were bad for us. At that time, you're statement sounded very reasonable.

"However, Eliza, the instructions coming from the touchstone are now very intense and speak only about being within the crystal room together before sunrise on the morning of the Summer Solstice. This is the thing which we are to do if we do not want to be lost from each other, forever. Please, Eliza, heed these instructions carefully. Meet Liz and I here at the adjoined tables before sunrise. We think that four AM would give us enough time to run to the north cliffs, slap the touchstone and shout, "I declare this run good and done.""

When Beth pauses, Liz says, "The touchstone has told me to hold onto those I want to stay with as we run and slap the stone. At that time, we'll go directly into the crystal room and Ann Anderson will meet us in there. While we're in the crystal room, we are to turn in one spot in the center of the room and sing the song that comes to us. If we do that, Eliza, the touchstone says that our dimensions will bond together for all our time on Earth."

Eliza says, "I haven't gone to the crystal room nor to Ann's dimension no matter what I do. I'll be here to go with you, I promise. I don't want to miss a chance to see either and I don't want to lose either of you. My runs to the north cliffs touchstone have been late in the afternoon, since Marie's death. I volunteer at the shop where I took my sister's things and don't get back until then. I love my work there. The shop's owner, Mary Trimble, has become a good friend and the work has been good for me. However, I'm want to meet Ann Anderson before the Solstice and I'm going to try to go through to her dimension today."

Liz says, "Why don't you just wait until you come with Beth and me on the Solstice next week? We'll slap the touchstone together and Ann will meet us in the crystal room. Please, Eliza, take these instructions seriously. They were given to Beth to keep us safe. Now I'm hearing them at my touchstone. Put your ear to your own stone to understand these instructions are for you, too. I know we don't know who gives us this information, but less serious warnings have come to each of us and proved true within days."

"I'm sorry if it seems we're jumping all over you, Eliza, but your lack of appearing at the adjoined tables has worried us. Do this for all of us, but especially yourself." Beth interjects. "Come here very early the morning of the Summer Solstice and we'll go together to the touchstone and the crystal cave. We must be in the crystal room before sunrise."

"Of course, my darlings. I am taking the warning about going into strange dimensions very seriously. In the last two weeks, I've had to slap my way back to my own dimension several times and never stay any longer than a few seconds. Trust me, I'll be very careful. However, right now, I'm going for my run. Afternoons on the beach are much quieter than the mornings. See you later."

As Eliza turns away, the other dimensions vanish and she slips out the slider door runs to the granite slab in record time. When she stands in front of the large protruding stone in the cliff face, she cheers, "My best time ever."

Facing the glowing stone, Eliza slaps it hard and shouts, "I declare this my best run ever, good and done." When nothing happens, she realizes how she changed the mantra and slaps the touchstone again, then shouts, "I declare this run good and done." Again, nothing seems to happen until she turns around and sees a spectacular vista spreading out miles to the south and west. A thick feral forest sweeps down a steep mountainside to end at the edge of a deep purple Pacific Ocean one mile below.

Stunned, she immediately turns and slaps the touchstone to return to her dimension. However, in the next instant, the ledge she stands upon suddenly raises a thousand feet upwards, leaving the thick forest far below her. Turning to the west, she sees only faint lines of waves beating against broken sea-stacks that march out from where the cliff point should be. The change is so dramatic it causes Eliza to recoil and press herself against the cliff face, shaking with fear.

Again, she turns to the golden stone in the cliff face and slaps it and screams, "I declare this run good and done." She is shocked when nothing happens and she yells, "Please, take me back. Take me home. I want my Redcliff's Beach."

The next moment, huge blocks of the granite cliff face break off and crash with thunderous noise into the forest far below. The resounding booms vibrate the ground as if earthquakes and the mountainside's thick forest sweeps down the slope in one massive landslide. When the dust settles, Eliza sees huge waves are crashing against the debris far below the ledge she stands upon.

Where the purple sea meets the slate grey of the sky, white puffy clouds pop from this horizon line and race to shore on a stiff wind. As these clouds sail over the cliff where Eliza cringes, she demands, "Why am I here? What did I do that sent me into this dimension? Damn, I changed the words when I slapped the touchstone that first time. But, I shouted the correct words the second time and third times. How could that have made so much difference? How many times do I have to slap the damned touchstone to get back home?"

Shaking her fist at the sky, she screams, "Take me home. I want to go back to my Redcliff's Beach. Do you hear me? I want my Redcliff's Beach. Take me back there right now."

Instantly, the dimension she is in becomes one of thousands of dimensions which spin and whirl around her. Pushing herself against the cliff face, Eliza is unable to look at the whirling mass without feeling sick, so she closes her eyes and shouts, "I declare this run good and done,"

Then she steps off the ledge and falls into the spinning abyss. A second later, she lands with a jarring thud and lies stunned for several minutes on a red granite surface. When she can sit up, she sees she is on a narrow sandy beach. Down the length of the beach are several perfectly sculpted dunes. Turning to look at the cliff face, she sees a familiar golden touchstone protruding from the granite. It looks exactly as the stone in her own Redcliff's Beach and she scrambles to her feet to touch the large glowing agate.

Overjoyed, Eliza stands in front of the stone and slaps the golden stone, shouting, "I declare this run good and done."

In the next moment, the touchstone moves out from the cliff face, lengthens to twelve feet long, slides down along the edge of the granite slab and digs its end into a boulder strewn rock covered beach. As she watches, steps appear in the length of the stone. Eliza is so relieved to see something which both Liz and Beth told her about that she exclaims, "I'm here. I'm at the touchstone stairs in Ann Anderson's dimension. Thank you, thank you, whoever did this. I thank you."

So sure she's in Ann Anderson's dimension, she expects to see Ann come down the path through the forest and wave to her from the edge of the shoreline. When Ann doesn't show up after several minutes, Eliza turns to the cliff face and sees a wide entrance has opened. Inside the opening, she sees a curving staircase with flashing light crossing the walls and ceiling.

"This is how Beth and Liz described the entrance up to the crystal room." Eliza shouts. "I didn't go to Ann's dimension, but I found the cave where the crystal room is. The others were so clear about what they saw here, I feel as if I've already been up those stairs. Now I get to discover that wonderful crystal room for myself. Ann Anderson, you're just going to have to wait to meet me next week on the Summer Solstice."

Laughing, Eliza hurries up the stairs without stopping until she reaches the wide entrance to the long hallway. Pausing only a few seconds, she hurries down the hall and passes the alcoves with the marble statues with only a glance into each. As she rushes on, determined to find the entrance into the giant geode, she shouts, "I'll look at those sculptures another time. Today I'm going straight to the crystal room."

As she hurries around the curve at the end of the hallway, Eliza gasps at the exquisite site before her. A wide opening covered with masses of tiny crystals which glitter brilliantly stops her and she shouts, "How beautiful. How absolutely beautiful."

Awe struck by the grand entrance of the giant geode, Eliza moves to touch the left side of the opening and touch the masses of tiny gems spread over it. Tinted many shades of blue and purples, the gems sparkle with a brilliance that nearly blinds her. A moment later, the light dims and she sees the massive room beyond the opening for a few seconds before brilliant explode through an opening in the cave's ceiling and nearly blinds her.

Covering her eyes, she peeks through the cracks between her fingers and sees thousands upon thousands of crystal formations of various shapes and sizes which flash the blinding light throughout the room. Closing her eyes again, she waits for the light to dim. When it does, she opens her eyes and looks up to the large hole in the cave's ceiling. Through it, she sees rafts of clouds skimming across a deep azure sky.

"Of course, it's brilliant when there's sun and dim when clouds cover it." She exclaims as if make a new discovery. Walking to the last large crystal blocking the entrance into the geode, she leans down and looks past the stone's largest facet and says, "Liz and Beth said there's a path of fire-opal tiles down there somewhere and it led them into that massive room."

Because of the dimness within the cave, it takes her eyes several seconds before she sees rich colors moving on the floor. Bending low, she realizes the colors are in the fire-opal tiles on a path. Following it around several large crystal formations and come to the edge of a wide circular floor and whispers,. "I've finally found you."

Instantly humbled by the vision before her, Eliza whispers, "Though Liz and Beth tried to explain this crystal room, they never came come close to how absolutely glorious this place truly is. No words can begin to describe it. This crystal room has to have come from another world."

Remembering what Beth and Liz said about hearing a song while turning in the center of the floor, Eliza goes to stand at the center of the circular floor and starts to slowly turn. As she turns, it seems the crystals move in the opposite direction while the colors within the fire-opal tiles swirl together causing a wondrous vortex of light and color which fills the room.

Closing her eyes, Eliza turns faster and a tune she has heard before comes into her mind. A gentle breeze wraps itself around her, then wafts through the crystal groupings causing the formations to vibrate harmonious tones which blend exquisitely with her singing. Spinning in tempo as the sounds fill her head, Eliza is dazzled by the brilliant effect and shouts, "I want to stay here forever. Do you hear me, whoever you are that created this special place? I want to stay here forever."

In the next second, Eliza is standing on a slab of red granite at the base of high red cliffs. Stunned by the sudden change of the dimensions, she looks around her and tries to understand what she said that made this change happen so fast. As she looks around, she is puzzled by what she sees and tells herself, "It looks familiar, but it's not my Redcliff's Beach. Those sand dunes are too few and too perfect. Yes, I've heard about this beach. It's Beth's beach. It's exactly as she's described her beach to Liz and me. Of course, it is and that silver trailer on the roundabout has to be Lucy Wong's. If that's Lucy's trailer, that must be Lucy coming down to the beach through the rip-rap. Yes, it is, she's thinks I'm Beth."

Waving to the woman running across the sand, Eliza calls out, "Hello there. It's good to see you." As she watches the woman run towards her, Eliza suddenly chokes out a loud sob and begins to cry, "Dear God, this must be what Heaven is. That's not Lucy. That's Marie running out to me. Darling Marie is alive and living here on Beth's beach! Yes, it is! Marie, my darling sister came to Beth's dimension when that plane crashed. How wonderful! Marie didn't die, she simply came into another dimension. That's what happens when we die? We just leave our dimension to go into another dimension. Thank you, dear God, thank you. Marie? Darling, I'm here. It's Eliza and I'm here."

Waving her hands over her head, Eliza steps off the slab of rock and starts towards the woman she believes is her sister. "Marie? Come here to the granite slab and let's slap our touchstone together. Let's be kids again and slap our touchstone together!"

As the other woman nears, Eliza turns to lead her sister onto the cliff face. However, at that moment, she is grabbed from behind and held so tight she is unable to pull away. Trying to turn to face the other woman, Eliza laughs loudly, "Marie, let go of me. I can't climb onto the slab if you hold me so tight. Let's hug in front of the touchstone before we slap it and shout, "I declare this run good and done."

Then, the woman holds her tighter and mumbles obscenities into Eliza's left ear. Reaching around behind the woman, Eliza tries to return what she assumes is a loving hug and squeezes the other woman as best she can and says, "My daring sister, I'm so thrilled to find you in this dimension. Are the twins here with you? You must be why I was sent here today. I was meant to find you here."

The woman holding her growls things so rapidly that Eliza is unable to understand her words until she tells about traveling days to find her. This so overjoys Eliza, that she cries out, "Yes, darling I know what you feel. I've missed you so much."

It's at this time, the woman's hands moves from her midsection to grasp Eliza's neck. Gasping for air, she rasps, "Please, Marie, I can't breathe. Let go of me!"

When the woman yanks Eliza's hair and pulls her head back, Eliza finally begins to twist and fight for each breath. Pushing backwards to move the woman away from her, Eliza cries out, "Marie, let go. I can't breathe. Let go...."

When a small space comes between the woman and herself, Eliza turns to look at the face of the woman holding her and sees it is not Marie. A rush of adrenaline flows through Eliza's body, as she gulps a breath, and screams, "You're not Marie. You're Beth's sister, Dee. You're Dee. You're the crazy one."

Terrified, Eliza swings wildly as her head is again pulled backwards and Eliza sees Dee's hate filled eyes. In that moment, she also feels a something move across her throat and her voice is silenced. Still, she pleads,

Please, Dee, let me go Dee, I'm not Beth. I'm Eliza Staples. I am not Beth. I'm not Beth. I'm Eliza Staples, Let me go. Let me go. You must let me go....

As her silent words tumble from her gaping mouth, Eliza feels something punch into her chest and hears, "Take that you stupid bitch. You're dead. I wanted to kill you years ago. Now I've done it. Nobody saved you this time."

As the last air leaves Eliza's body, Dee screams, "Take this, you damn bitch."

Then something sharp slides deep into Eliza's heart and her body falls against the person holding on to her, then falls face down onto the sand. Instantly, she is in a tunnel of white light and the large white dog says to her,

My name is Karma.

THIRTEEN

June 20ᵗʰ—The Summer Solstice

LIZ and **Beth** run to the north cliffs holding each other's hands. Both of their animal familiars, Kip and Dandelion, race ahead of them, playing tag as they bound along the beach. When the two women reach the granite slab, the two animals are waiting for them beneath the glowing touchstone. Pleased that they beat the rising sun by several minutes, the women raise their joined hands and slap the large golden agate together, shouting, "I declare this run good and done."

Expecting the entrance to the curving stairs to open, they are delighted when they find themselves, and their animals, in the very center of the crystal room. Looking around the gently glowing room, Liz exclaims, "We did it, Beth. We're in the crystal room before sunrise on the Summer Solstice. Let's hope that Ann keeps her promise to get here on time."

At hearing Ann's name, Kip barks three times, runs up the stairs and out through the opening in the cave's ceiling. Almost immediately, the smiling dog returns with Ann's Honey following right behind him. Seconds later, their Parallel Life known as Ann Anderson hurries down the stairs and shouts her greetings to Beth and Liz. "You're here. I beat the sunrise only a few minutes but I made it. I was so relieved when Kip came out and met us, as it told me you were ahead of me."

Laughing, Beth says, "And now we'll all stay together for the rest of our lives and be able to celebrate each Summer Solstice down here in this beautiful crystal room. Before the sun rises, let's thank the people who found the giant geode and created this amazing crystal room."

"Also, let's celebrate the original child know as Elizabeth Ann Anderson who gave each of us a new life. Aren't we amazing?" Ann says as she reaches the other women in the center of the fire-opal floor and says, "Let's celebrate being together, as that's what really counts today, the three of us."

Hugging Ann, Liz says, "I wouldn't have missed being here with you both for anything in the world."

Beth agrees and says, "Let's also celebrate having known Eliza Staples for the past year and say a prayer for her travels to her next life."

Looking at them sheepishly, Ann says, "I came down to do my daily meditation on the crystal thrones and only remembered it was our day to be together when I heard Kip bark and Honey took off. Please, don't be mad at me. I've been so busy building my cabin over the golden stone that my mind is still stuck out there."

Seeing the questioning looks on the women's faces, Ann stops and stares at them for several seconds. Then she says, "Oh, didn't I tell you about my meditating here on one of the crystal thrones? Didn't I?"

Shaking her head, Liz says, "No, Ann, you didn't. At least, not to me. You're actually admitting that you come in here every morning and sit on one of those thrones to meditate?"

"Yes. I started it right after I found the cave when I was a small child. The first time I crawled in was through a hole that was hardly big enough for me to squeeze through, so it was easy to hide from others. I used it for years, whenever I could slip away from Dana and my folks. When she turned thirteen and discovered boys, I was able to explore the cave for longer periods of time. That's when I found the stairs up to the opening in the cave's ceiling. From then on, I simply walked down the stairs into the cave. The same berm, with the tall grasses, that hides it today, hid it at that time. I've avoided creating a path by using different routes over the berm."

"It's interesting to hear you say how much freedom your parents gave you." Liz says, "My folks never allowed Dana Marie and I go past the granite slab. They let us use the south beach as far as we wanted to go. We only ran to the north cliffs to slap our touchstone. As for the cliff tops, I never even thought of going up there. I think Dana did with her friends, but just to go over to the small beach for bonfires. My friends were more interested in the skating rink and the games in the town center."

Beth agrees, "Before she hit her head and got weird, Dee climbed all over the cliffs. It drove our folks sick with worry as they were sure they'd find her body washed up on the beach or flattened out on the granite slab. She'd scramble along the ledges like a mountain goat. After the accident she became terrified of heights and even stopped running to the touchstone with me and our folks. I never heard her say anything about finding a hole or cave."

"As far as I know, no one else in this dimension found it. I was able to buy the cliffs and the steep forest where I built my house. Even now, I never climb the berm in the same place to keep from making paths through the grasses. Once the cliff face fell and blocked the entrance into the stairwell, I've made certain it never shows from the outside. I've had this wonderful room to myself for years and I'm not ready to share it with anyone. At least not in my own dimension. I was shocked when you two showed up."

Then, as if trying to change the subject, Ann points to the far side of the cave and exclaims, "Hey, look at the crystals on the wall to the left of the thrones. Is that woman the one you called Eliza? The one that was killed by Beth's sister last week?"

Staring at the crystals next to the thrones, Beth sees nothing unusual and says, "Eliza's not here, Ann. She died a week ago. I told you right after it happened."

"I know that, Beth," Ann snaps, "But there's a woman's image amongst the crystals to the left side of the thrones. See? There, just above the stone bench a few feet away from the nearest crystal where the thrones are. Don't you see the colors amongst the crystals on the wall?"

Peering through the dim light, Liz points, "I see what you mean. That area of colors within the crystals above the stone bench? Yes, I see it. Look, Dandy's pawing at it as if chasing a moth and trying to catch it. It's a shadow of a person."

Holding up her hands, Beth shakes her head, "Whoa, you two. I don't see anyone else in here. Today is too cloudy and the light's too dim. I think your eyes are playing tricks on you. It would be nice if it weren't so overcast today. A few sun breaks would be nice to have."

A second after she says this, sunlight spills through the opening in the ceiling of the cave and the crystals explode with brilliant flashing light. That's when Beth exclaims, "I see her, Ann. It is Eliza and that white dog that came to her after Marie died, is sitting right next to her on the stone bench. Is that the dog you saw in her home, Liz? Look, Kip and Dandelion are touching noses with it."

As soon as she speaks, Beth crosses the room and stands in front of the image, crying out, "Eliza, dear Eliza, how wonderful it is to see you again. I'm so sorry Dee mistook you for me. It was me she meant to kill. Not you. Never you."

"Are you here to be with us on the Summer Solstice?" Liz asks. When there is no response from the image, she says, "Beth, let's sit here on the bench and tell Ann all we remember about Eliza. That will tell Eliza know how much she meant to us and how sorry she is gone. Maybe her essence will stay with us for the day."

Sitting on the stone bench next to the image within the crystals on the wall, Liz turns to Ann and shares her memories of Eliza Staples and, when she finishes, Beth does the same. As the women talk about the woman they knew as Eliza Staples, the image becomes more of a shape than a shadow. Then the image settles on the bench beside the white dog and wraps its arms around the large animal..

Stunned, by this show of affection by Eliza's image, both Liz and Beth begin to weep and, when their animal familiars see this, they move next to their mistresses, put their snouts in the air and begin to howl in low mournful tones. Then Dandelion sits up between Beth's feet and begins to caterwaul loudly with the other animals.

Soon, the animals' howling grows so loud that Liz turns her face up to the cave's ceiling and begins howling along with the animals. Immediately, the two other women join her and the combined howls reverberate through the massive room causing the crystals within the room to vibrate at a different pitches. The resulting harmonic hum fills the room with a wondrous energy and the three animals suddenly stop their howling and race up the stairs to the outside.

Laughing, Beth says, "I think the crystals' vibrations got too much for their ears. I know it was getting to mine. Though, honestly, wasn't the howling a great release? Didn't it make you feel good? We're so lucky to have those wonderful animals in our lives. What would we do without their being here to lighten our mood?"

"I know what you mean, Beth. Honey keeps me going through my darkest times. It's as if she knows when I need to lighten up or could use a good laugh. I don't know what I'd do without her." Ann admits as she wipes her tears on her sleeve. "I'm so glad she has Kip and Dandy as friends and that I have you and Beth in my life. I want you both to know how lucky I feel to have met you both. It's a true blessing to share my amazing cave with you."

Beth nods, "Our luck really started when Dad found the touchstone and put that part of it in the floor of his cabin. It's that stone that connects us and brought us to this amazing place. It was that same touchstone that told me I was the original Elizabeth Ann Anderson and that I was responsible to bring the Parallel Lives of Elizabeth Ann to this place every Summer Solstice. I took that to mean there are other Parallel Lives of Elizabeth Ann Anderson that are living in other dimensions. The stone didn't give me any idea as how we'll find them. So I guess that's up to the three of us."

"I've been wondering if there are anymore of us." Ann tells her. "Other than you two, I've never seen anyone like me, but I've always felt as if there were someone waiting for me to find them. Have either of you? Liz?"

"No, I've not. Eliza saw another of us once. That woman ran right through her and went into a tunnel through the cliffs to a beach with golden sand. She was quite shaken by the whole thing." Liz says, "I have often wondered where those messages come from which Beth and I get from the touchstone. Who's behind them and what are their intentions?"

At that time, Beth says "Listening to the touchstone every day has become a responsibility that I really don't like. Now I'm sure the last warning was for Eliza as it foretold her death. I will always tell you exactly what the messages are. Each of us must listen to the touchstone and take responsibility to follow them on our own volition. Did Eliza understand how serious the last message was for all of us?"

Liz replies, "I heard her say she understood, yet for some reason, she stayed too long in your dimension. You can't take responsibility for her actions, Beth. After you told us the touchstones message, I asked the stone myself and was given the same information you told Eliza and me. Just because you are the original child, you are not responsible for her actions nor for her death. It was Eliza who got herself killed, no one else is to blame."

"Yes, Beth, Liz is right. Eliza is the only one who could have slapped the touchstone to change dimensions and save herself." Ann agrees.

Liz says, "Marie died only weeks ago. When Eliza saw Dee running to her, she must have thought it was her sister. Our minds do funny things when we've lost loved ones."

"Okay, you two. Nothing will change what happened or explain why Eliza didn't do what she needed to return to her own dimension," Beth exclaims. "Let's enjoy being together in the crystal room on the Summer Solstice."

Suddenly the animals run back through the opening from the outside and down to where the three women sit. Standing in front of Liz, Kip barks three times and then his words fill Liz's mind,

Eliza wants to thanks you for coming here today.

Shouting for the others to listen to what he says, they turn and see that Eliza's image is again within the crystals on the wall. Stepping closer to it, Liz says, "Thank you for coming to be with us on this Summer Solstice, Eliza. Will you tell Kip what happened the day you died? He will tell me what you say and I'll tell the others. Please, tell us what happened."

For the next hour, Eliza tells of her experiences on the day of her death,

My dear Parallel Lives of Elizabeth Ann Andersons, It's wonderful to be with you in the crystal room on this Summer Solstice. Know that Kip is an old friend from many lifetimes as are Honey and Dandelion. Do not mourn for me, my dear friends. I saw Marie in Dee. There was nothing anyone could have changed. The ending to my life was written on the day of my birth. Know that no mortal action can change a destiny.

Eliza then tells them how she knew it was Beth's dimension but when she saw Dee she wanted more than anything for her to be Marie. As she speaks, Kip tells Liz and Liz tells the others what she says. When Eliza pauses or seems to have finished her story, the three women begin speaking amongst themselves. Four times, Kip needs to bark to hush them so Eliza's words can be heard and told. Finally, she says,

Tell Ann Anderson that I'm glad she came with Honey. It is good to see the three animal familiars again. They have each brought much joy to my past lives. Know that all the Elizabeth Ann Andersons are blessed children. The white dog's name is Karma. He will deliver me to the life I am to relive to learn total humility. In it, I will receive as great a harm as I gave harming others, in this lifetime. Know that I will never hurt another soul in any life I will ever live. My time with you brought me much joy. Now I must leave for it is time to follow Karma to my next life. I give you my love and gratitude. Goodbye.

After her last words, Eliza's image fades into the crystals on the wall until the colors are no longer visible. Though they no longer see her, the three women stare at where her image had been for several minutes. Finally, Beth turns and walks to the center of the fire-opal floor and calls to the others, "Come over here. Let's turn in the center of the floor and sing the crystal room's song for Eliza. Then she'll know how much she was loved by us."

Beth begins to turn in the very center of the fire-opal tiled floor. Liz and Ann rush to stand on either side of her and begin to turn in tempo with her turns. Soon music fills their heads and their voices blend in a perfection no one has heard before. As their singing becomes louder, the crystal room vibrates with soft tones that blend perfectly with their voices.

As the music enfolds the women, each falls into a trance and slips slowly to the floor where they lie flat on their backs upon the fire-opal tiles. Seeing their mistress on the floor, each animal familiar goes to her and snuggles against the sleeping woman.

It is a slit of brilliant light that slowly appears at the far edge of the fire-opal tiles, exactly below the crystal thrones, which causes the three animals sit up and watch. When the phantom opening if fully expanded, a golden staircase rises from inside until it is level with the fire-opal tiles on the floor. Then gliding up from the opening, two exquisite entities appear at the top of the stairs and greet the three animals as if old friends.

Instantly, the animals run to greet the entities stepping onto the fire-opal tiled floor and create a great joyful noise of recognition. When the two entities become fully formed and solid, they hug each of the animals and greet them by name. Then, one points towards the women lying on the floor and asks each animal to introduce its mistress. As this is done, the entities listen with great interest to what each animal has to say about their mistress.

After each animal has spoken, the two beings move around the three lying on the floor and rejoice in what they see. It is during this time that each entity becomes the human that they are to be, male and female, tall and slender in form with a royal stance and presumed attitude. The tallest is a handsome very fit elder man shorn of all hair showing a perfect skull under his tanned skin. He wears silk cloaks of many shades of purple over his body and a glittering crown of spun gold upon his head.

The other entity is an elegant woman with thick white braids wrapping her head several times and complimenting her golden skin. Over her tall body she wears silken sheaths of hues of azure blues.

Wrapping her head is a golden chain holding a fist sized diamond at her forehead.

In each of their right hands, the entities hold long golden staffs topped with a large globes encrusted with many jewels. As they circle the three women and their familiars on the floor, the entities touch each three times and ask the familiars to tell the woman how pleased they are by what they see.

Finally the man stops and the woman comes to his side and takes his hand. Both stand silently looking down at the women with loving adoration. Turning to the man, the woman says, "James, aren't you glad that our Elizabeth Ann came to the crystal room as I asked her to do. I know you thought it was too soon to see her. However, with the death of the one called Eliza, we had to come for her and it is so nice to see the wonderful results of these other three. Don't you agree?"

"Yes, it pleases me very much to see her. I wonder if she'll guess who made the request to meet us here." While he speaks, Kip and Honey wag their tails and Dandelion purrs loudly. This cause the woman to look down at the animals and say, "Kip, it has been so good to see you again. You, too, Honey. And especially you, Dandelion. I am so pleased that you three joined your mistresses to meet us here today. You must be very proud of them. It seems that they have become wonderful people. Each of you must tell her how pleased we are of our Elizabeth Ann. Aren't we, James?"

Nodding, James, adds, "Jill is right. We are very pleased. You have been excellent familiars to each one you brought today. Our journey through the wormhole was long and arduous and, when we heard your adjoined howls, it lightened our journey and gave us much joy. It showed how appreciated each of you are by your mistress. Dandelion, it is good that you did show your true self today. You must wait until next Earth's Summer Solstice when the Parallel Lives of Elizabeth Ann have fully gathered."

Laughing, Jill says, "Yes, indeed. Then, you may all show off your true selves and become adjoined again. Do we know how many are yet to be collected, James? Will their familiars lead them to the crystal room, as these have done?"

"Yes, darling Jill, all is set and in the works. You must be patient. Some Parallel Lives no longer have connections to the cabin or to Redcliff's Beach. These will find their own way to the crystal room. By Summer Solstice, next Earth year, all will be with us in one form or another as it will be the year of Elizabeth Ann's Saturn Return. What a joyous happening it will be to have our daughters, Dana Marie and Elizabeth Ann, home with us again."

Raising the long golden staff, James tips it so that the jeweled globe touches the head of each animal and tells them, "Know you are powerful and are to nudge your familiars when necessary to keep them from wandering. They have many lessons to learn in one short Earth year. But, it will be done. Now, dear friends, Jill and I must say goodbye as it is time for us to leave you. Allow your mistresses the freedom to discover what they must by the next time we meet. We look forward to seeing you all on that day."

Jill agrees, "They are as infants as they learn to move between dimensions, so be patient with them. Let them make discoveries as often as possible. We will continue feeding needed information through the touchstones. You will each know what is to come before they do."

Smiling, James takes Jill's hand and kisses it, saying "Look at our beautiful girls, Jill. Didn't we create wonderful entities?"

Jill's eyes shine bright with the pride of a loving parents as she replies, "Yes, these are as they should be. It was Eliza who was the lost one and we must help Karma deliver her soul to the new life he has chosen for her."

Patting each animal on its head, James says, "Wake your mistresses as soon as we're leaving. Let them see us go. Tell them who we are and that we are very pleased with what we saw. Watch over them. We'll see you on next Earth year's Summer Solstice. Now, we must return to U-ran-o-sis through the wormhole."

The man puts his arm around the woman's waist and pulls her to his side, "Don't cry, Jill, we'll see our Elizabeth in one short Earth year. Our Dana Marie will gather with us at that time. It is a short Earth year and that is very soon."

"Soon enough, James, darling. Let us collect Eliza and Karma. It's time to move her to her new life. And Dee, the poor thing, I'm certain she is so hot where she had to go."

"Yes, Karma sent Dee to suffer two lowly lifetimes. She'll not be happy when we next see her. Let's leave our staffs at the crystal thrones, where we were joined as one. The staffs will show Elizabeth Ann that she is a cherished child and has never been forgotten."

"You're so kind, my dear. Hurry, Karma, bring Eliza to the wormhole. We must go quickly. Elizabeth Ann is stirring. Quickly. Quickly, you two. Follow us into the worm hole. Eliza, you must go ahead and let Karma lead you to your new life."

As the entities go down the staircase, the large wormhole slowly closes. At that exact moment, the three women sit up and look across the room to see the images of James, Jill, Eliza and Karma disappearing down the wormhole.

Liz shouts, "What is that?"

Neither Beth nor Ann answer her, but scramble to their feet and run to where the brilliantly lit wormhole grows smaller until it vanishes. When it does, Beth shouts, "Mommy wait for me. Come back, Mommy. Please. Daddy. Come back." Then she turns to the others and says, "I saw my Mother and Father. I would recognize them anywhere. Eliza was with them. Wasn't she?"

"Yes, she was. And that white dog was too. They must have come while we lay on the floor. Can you see where they disappeared?" Liz shouts as she throws herself at the base of the crystal thrones.

Kneeling on the floor beside her, Ann says, "The opening closed. I don't see how they could have come through these tiles. What do you think we saw?"

Not having an explanation, the three women simply stare at the bottom edge of the crystal thrones and the fire-opal tiles that meet it on the floor. Then Ann shouts, "Look what's leaning between the crystal thrones. Were those staffs leaning there when we came this morning?"

"No. I'm sure they weren't." Beth says and takes the tallest one in her right hand. "I saw this staff in that dream I had the first time I came to the crystal room. That couple must have been our parents and they came to take Eliza home with them. They left their staffs for us so we'd know they were here. Yes, this other one is exactly like the staff the elegant woman held up for me to take. When I did, I set it beside the man on the other throne beside me. Rurik from U-ran-o-sis was his name. All the people cheered and raised their own gilded staffs high over their heads. Though none of the other staffs were covered with jewels, it was very exciting."

Taking hold of the other staff with her right hand, Liz demands, "What the hell happened to us? My watch says we slept for over two hours. Did that happened while we were spinning and singing or what?"

Ann replies, "No, I don't think we were asleep. I think we were put in a trance. I still have a rather fuzzy feeling. Do either of you? It happened after our voices harmonized as we sang together. Wasn't it amazing?"

"Yes, it was. I wonder if the animals saw what happened or if they fell asleep at the same time we did. Kip, did you fall asleep or did you see what happened?" Liz asks the dog.

We slept beside you until Jill and James Anderson came through the wormhole to view you and collect Eliza's soul. They said to tell you they are very proud of the three of you and look forward to seeing you next year at this time. You will meet more Parallel Lives of Elizabeth Ann before then and you will bring them here so they can gather within this crystal room. We're all to return here on the next Summer Solstice.

"Oh my-gosh!" Liz cries out, staring at Kip. "Beth, Ann, listen to what Kip just said..." After she repeats Kip's words, the three women look around the crystal room, as if trying to find something they've lost.

Ann says, "Do you think they're still in the room with us?"

Without being asked, Kip responds,

No, they were the images you saw going into the wormhole. They are now over halfway to their home on U-ran-o-sis. Wormholes are conduits that allow travelers to cross light years of space in nanoseconds. These conduits come from somewhere in this universe to anywhere in other universe. Our Earth is one of billions of planets where humanoids are able to live on the zillions of known universes.

James and Jill return to Earth each Summer Solstice to check on the development of their daughters, Dana Marie and Elizabeth Ann. Today, they came to take the soul of Eliza Staples to where she will relive the life and feel great harm to be lived through. You will meet your parents the year of your Saturn Return. At time they will take you home to U-ran-o-sis.

After Liz repeats Kip's information, Ann shouts, "You mean that our parents came here through a wormhole conduit from another planet? U-ran-o-sis? What does he mean they come every year? What's a Saturn Return? When we go with them, will we be dead or alive?"

Liz looks at Kip without repeating Ann's questions.

On your Saturn Return, they will meet with you in the crystal room where each of the Parallel Lives from Dana Marie and Elizabeth Ann will gather to their original child during Earth's Summer Solstice. Until then, each of, you will continue to live as you have intended. You are to be true to yourself and enjoy your time on Earth. When you are to meet new Elizabeth Ann's and gather them to you.

Liz repeats Kip's message. For several minutes, the women stay silent, lost in their own thoughts until Ann starts to speak again. Shouting over her, Beth says, "Stop asking questions, Ann. We've enough to think about. James and Jill Anderson were here and left their golden staffs. This next year we're to meet more of our Parallel Lives. We have enough to think about. Do either one of you even know what a Saturn Return is?"

When she finishes her tirade, Beth begins walking through the crystal cave and looking into the deepest corners of the room. Without a word, Liz goes in another direction and Ann does the same. For the next hour, the animals lay on the fire-opal tiles in the middle of the floor and watch their mistresses cross each other's paths as they move to and fro through the massive room checking and rechecking around each crystal grouping as they search for answers to something they won't ever understand.

Finally, Liz stops beside Kip, who sits in the center of the room with Honey and Dandy, and says to Beth and Ann, "Let's sit here with our familiars and ask other Parallel Lives of Elizabeth Ann to come to this crystal room and be with us this coming year. If we keep asking, maybe they will hear us and come to us. It certainly can't hurt to ask, can it? Then, let's pray for the safe return of our parents as they journey back to U-ran-o-sis and thank them for coming to see us."

After their silent prayers have been sent out to the Universe, Liz lifts her head and asks, "Kip? Were our parents pleased when they saw us?"

Yes, they said they were very proud of the women you've become.

Beth stands and says, "Let's leave the staffs where we found them and go out to see what Ann has done on the cabin over her golden stone?"

"Okay. But first, let's slap the largest jeweled globes and shout our mantra for good luck." Liz suggests. So the three women stand in front of the long staffs with the jewel encrusted globes and raise their right hands. Then as if one, they slap each globe then shout, "I declare this run good and done."

AUGUST EPILOGE

LIZ and Kip rush through the slider door and find Beth, Dandy, Ann and Honey all sitting around their adjoined tables. "Hey everyone, it's great to see you're here. Did you run to the north cliffs this morning?" she asks watching Kip tuck himself beside Dandy and Honey on the golden stone under the table.

"Not yet. Ann stayed at my house last night so we're having a late morning. We'll run after we talk with you. Go get your coffee and come sit. We have something to tell you."

Liz grins as she fills her coffee mug, then sits on her favorite chair. "Okay, what's up with you two?"

Ann puts her hand on Beth's arm and says, "Let me tell her, Beth. After all, I was the one who made the first move."

Beth smiles at her and nods, "We want to be honest with you, Liz. There shouldn't be any secrets between us. We three are one and the same in many ways. However, Ann and I are different from you in our unique way. Just know that we both love and adore you, though just not the same as we love and adore each other."

In answer to that, Liz laughs loud and long. When she finally quiets to a chuckle, she says, "Well, ladies, I figured that out weeks ago. So tell something new. Are you going to move into one house and abandon the other?"

Ann smiles and replies, "No, we'll use both depending on what is going on it each of our lives. My sister Dana Marie comes for visits often and I want to keep our relationship strong. Beth has friends and nieces that mean a lot to her also. Mostly, we'll play it by ear and go with the flow, as they say. That's all I have to say. Beth, do you want to jump in and give anything more away before I do?"

Beth looks puzzled and says, "What? I didn't tell what happened. Did I, Liz?"

Getting up from her chair, Liz goes around the table to give the two a hug and says, "Congratulations you two, though I'm not really surprised. You two have been spending a lot of time together and there felt more to it than getting Ann's cabin built. Now, this is the perfect time to update you on what's been going on in my life. Do you remember what I told you about becoming more than interested in Kip's veterinarian? Well, here's the ending of that short happy story..."

At that time, Liz tells them about the evening Larry Jackson asked a couple questions and how she told the whole truth about who and what she it. Then she tells of Dr. Dan Parker's non-reaction and how the Jacksons reacted to everything. "I didn't say anything to either of you at the time, as I wanted to give Dan time to think it over and come talk with me if he wanted. Well, the good Dr. didn't. I've not heard one word nor have the Jacksons. Dr. Dan Parker dropped from our lives totally. The Jacksons are quite bitter about how he's acted.

"In many way, I am relieved that he showed us his real self before Kip and I got more deeply involved with him. Since then, my life has gone better than ever and I'm wiser woman for having known him. Now I'm ready for whoever and whatever comes at me in the future. Who knows what'll happen by the next Summer Solstice."

Printed in the United States
By Bookmasters